Farr House

Past is Present

The Second Book in the Farr Family Saga

Anita D. Boseman

ISBN: 979-8-88945-002-3
eISBN: 979-8-88945-003-0

Brilliant Books Literary
137 Forest Park Lane Thomasville
North Carolina 27360 USA

Printed in the United States of America

Acknowledgements

This book is dedicated to my late husband Vann for putting up with my prolonged bursts of writing and to my sister, Carolyn, who is my primary editor and greatest fan.

This is also a work of fiction. None of the characters, events, etc. are real, it's all just a figment of my very active imagination! Enjoy!

Contents

Home in Houston

Melody Fitzhugh Farr turned the key in the lock of the heavy oak door. It swung silently inward at her light touch. Putting her carryon down on the foyer table, Melody hurried across the room to the security panel to punch in the code.

Flipping on the lights, the entryway of her home came to life with a blaze of light. Gina Russel, Melody's best friend, struggled through the door with several bags from the duty-free zone in Schiphol Airport.

"My heavens, girl, did you leave anything behind for other people?" Gina lightly teased Melody. "I would never have recommended you go through Amsterdam on your way home if I thought you were going to clear out their duty-free shops!"

Melody and Gina had met and became friends on the first week of college almost ten years ago. When Melody told Gina of her plans to come home for Thanksgiving and Christmas, Gina had told her the best thing to do was take the slight side-trip through Amsterdam's airport and their shopping zone. From the number of packages, it looked like Melody had fared quite well.

Melody smiled, "You know I hate to shop, but I just couldn't pass up some of the things in the grocery. Droste's cocoa, French chestnuts, marzipan shaped into Christmas ornaments, and I hated having to leave some of the beautiful fruit behind. However, customs here frowns on bringing it in." Melody reached out to take some of the bags from Gina. "Come on through to the kitchen and we'll have some wine while I put this stuff away."

In the kitchen, Gina took a bottle of wine from the small wine cooler under the kitchen island and poured glasses for both of them. "You know, I have missed this place." Gina said as she looked around her. "Every time I would pass the gate while you were gone I would remember some holiday or another that you, your mother, and I would spend the day cooking for and then taking the food across the street to the church for the homeless to eat. It is great having you back so we don't miss that this year."

Melody nodded, "Yes, but this will be the first year without Mother and it makes me miss her all the more. It was so different in Farr Cottage. I didn't see her in every room, in the village, or at church. Here, well, she's everywhere."

"However," Melody continued, "it is so wonderful being back home and I don't mind the memories of her. Having her in my heart will keep Mother always with me."

While the two talked, Melody was busy putting the things she had bought in the airport away. One item in particular caught Gina's eye. "Could you have gotten a bigger tin of cocoa? What will you do with all of that?"

Laughing, Melody kidded her, "It will probably go into those mousse cakes you like so much or the pecan chocolate cakes covered in ganache we have for your birthday! Remember, Christmas is coming up. And there is fudge to make, rum/chocolate balls to roll, and hot cocoa on Christmas morning after church. I'm worried there won't be enough!"

Before the girls had finished their wine, the items were put away. Melody turned to Gina. Come on up and visit while I put the other things away."

Gina shook her head and put the half-empty glass on the sink, "Nope, can't tonight. Or is it this morning? I have to be in the office first thing. We have people coming in from Korea with some new fabric designs and I have to be there to approve them."

"OK, but keep me in mind. If they have any blouse or dress weight silk you think I might like, take a swatch. Louisa needs to make me some things before I go back to England and I need to get the fabric."

Gina turned to look at her friend. "Do you have to go back there? You just got home, haven't even unpacked, and already have plans to leave. What is so important at this Farr Cottage?" Then she smiled. "Or should I ask *who* is so important at Farr Cottage?"

Melody blushed. "Look, you have an early day tomorrow and I'm in need of some sleep. We can talk about this another time. OK?"

Gina looked closely at her friend. She had caught the blush, and now she was ready to forget her obligations to the foreign merchants. However, Melody was already punching in the security code to turn off the system while she left. "Fair enough, but you need to tell me all about him, it, or whatever. How about brunch on Saturday? I'm free then, and you should be over any jet lag. How about it?"

Melody nodded. "I'll make it here and we can spend most of the day talking. Drive carefully."

Gina left. Melody slid a discreet panel above the alarm keypad up to reveal a security monitor. She watched the gate for her friend to exit, and then Melody set the alarm for both the house and grounds. Closing the panel, she took her bag from the table where she had left it, grabbed her purse, and turned off the lights.

A motion sensor in the pin-lights along the left stairway provided some muted illumination for her to ascend the stairs to her bedroom. The lights had been put in for her grandmother's convenience and were a wonderful idea. As Melody turned into the hall where her bedroom was, she felt a pang of sadness as she passed the closed door to the suite that had been her mother's.

Melody had seen pictures of the original house that her great-great-grandfather had built. But a hurricane had damaged much of it, and the house was totally rebuilt and the remaining parts redesigned by her great-grandfather, Avery Farr. The result was a grand house much like one he had seen on a trip to Italy when he and his bride were on their honeymoon.

Great-great-grandfather Richard and his wife, Lucy, had a private suite at the end of the opposing hall, but the rooms her great-grandfather, Avery, had shared with his wife, Constance, were located at the end of the hall where her bedroom was. When her grandfather, Charles Farr, had married, Richard and Lucy had already passed away, and their rooms were taken by Charles and his wife. Her grandmother raised Melody's dad in this house, and she died in her bedroom. As each suite of rooms became vacant through, first, the death of her great-grandparents, then her grandmother, and now her mother, the rooms were simply closed and left as they were.

The door to Melody's room was open, and light from a full moon partially illuminated it for her. She flipped on the light switch and let out a sigh of relief at finally being home.

Her favorite color was blue, and the room had been redone as a present for her graduation when she had received her master's degree. She had always wanted a canopy bed, but the four-poster that she finally chose was more open. A seating area in front of the fireplace had a lovely blue and cream-striped sofa, two solid blue chairs, and plenty of cushions. The area was finished with some convenient tables where she could put her books and a cup of tea.

The room had an ample closet, a design feature for which she had her great-grandmother to thank, and a roomy bath. The floors were parquet topped by carpets. The closet had built-in dressers, so the only other furniture in her room, beside the things in the seating area, was a dressing table, a desk, and her nightstands.

Melody set about unpacking the small bag she had taken with her on the plane. She had sent her other bags and boxes ahead by UPS, and they should arrive in the morning.

While she dressed for bed, Melody smiled as she remembered the first night she had spent in the servants' quarters of Farr Cottage. The comfortable bed in her room in Farr House was a totally different affair from the narrow, squeaky cot in which she had tried to fall asleep. It wasn't until Melody's guardian, Arthur, had returned from a trip that her room was changed and more normal accommodations made for her.

However, like that first night in Farr Cottage, Melody found sleep difficult. Her mind replayed the last few days she had been in England, starting with the morning after Lord Alfred's dinner party.

Lord Arthur Farr, Viscount of Gibbons, had made arrangements for her, his ward, to return to her home in Houston. Something about the way he treated her at breakfast that morning made her wonder if he was trying to be rid of her. The travel arrangements he had made gave her little time to eat, pack, and get to the train station to go back to the Cottage.

As she came down the stairs of the London house, her guardian stood in the door and urged her to hurry. A black taxi sat waiting for her, and the cabbie put her suitcases in the trunk. However, before she left, her cousin hugged her and planted a kiss on her cheek, something he had never done before. Then, he hurried her into the cab just as her friend, Lord Alfred Oswin, was coming across the street, calling her name. Melody turned to look out the back window and saw the two men, Arthur and Alfred, arguing on the street.

John, Lord Arthur's employee from Farr Cottage was waiting for her at the station when she arrived in the village. Nedda, his wife, and the housekeeper at the Cottage, had already packed most of her clothes by the time she got there. Melody had the distinct impression her cousin was trying to get her on her way.

That evening, fresh off the train from London, Alfred arrived. Nedda didn't want to let him in when he knocked on the door, but Melody was in the library and heard the commotion. She welcomed him and asked Nedda to bring tea to the sitting room.

Something had changed. Alfred seemed nervous and Melody asked him what the problem was. "You and Arthur are always at each other. Sometimes the two of you act no better than a couple of kids fighting over the same toy."

Alfred looked at her. "You don't know how close to right you are. There has always been a tension between us, it goes back to a relative we do or don't have in common, but it's worse than that. Now, it seems we are both interested in the same girl, and neither of us has been in this kind of situation before."

Melody was surprised. *A girl or woman? Hmm.* She hadn't seen Arthur or Alfred in the company of anyone since she had arrived. *Who could it be? She wondered.* She didn't know about Alfred. But as for Arthur, when he was here in the country, she rarely saw him leave the house, much less mixing or dating anyone.

"Is that what your argument was about this morning? I saw the two of you standing in the street as my taxi was leaving and I was worried you might hit each other. Were you arguing about this woman or just rubbing each other up the wrong way as usual?

"Actually, we were arguing about you." He rushed on before she could respond. "Melody, you must know that I care for you as a friend, but what hit me last night was you are much more than that to me. You're important in my life." He looked at her and grinned. "Whoof! There, I've said it. Uh … what I mean to say is, last night I realized you are … well … I'll miss you, and I don't want you to leave."

Melody started to speak, but he rushed ahead. "I knew Arthur was going to be down on the idea, but it was much more than even I expected. It turns out, I was not the only one to have the same epiphany, and it seems he also decided last night he had feelings for you."

As surprising as the first declaration of affection had been, the second piece of news left Melody without words. Alfred kept talking, but Melody was unable to hear what he was saying. *Arthur and Alfred? Impossible!* She would leave for Houston as soon as she could make arrangements.

Alfred finally broke through to her, "Please have lunch with me tomorrow. I want to spend some time with you before you leave. Please say yes."

Half thinking, Melody agreed and Alfred left.

Setting her cold tea on the cart, Melody went up to her room. She had arrangements to make.

The quickest flight Melody could find was late the next evening. Her friend, Gina, had mentioned Amsterdam to her on one of their late-night online chat sessions, and flights to that international hub left quite regularly. Instead of going through London, Melody would take the train to an airport just south of the city, then it was a short flight to Schiphol, spend a couple of hours in the transit lounge, and finally, a KLM flight directly to Houston.

Before she went to sleep, the necessary e-mails had been sent to the travel agent in London, who had originally issued the tickets, a notice to the bank in Houston that she was returning on a different date than previously arranged, and a short note to Gina. Her friend would be at the airport to get her when she landed.

With the plans and preparations made, she slept fitfully. Her dreams were filled with Alfred and Arthur. By morning, her mind was still in a muddle.

Alfred arrived to take Melody to lunch just as the familiar brown truck of UPS was departing with her luggage. Rather than leave the house and be alone with Alfred, Melody asked him to stay and eat in the dining room. Reluctantly, he agreed. However, he had hoped to get her away from the prying eyes of Arthur's housekeeper, Nedda.

Melody finally drifted off to sleep, but her dreams were occupied with the two men who were attracted to her.

Melody's room had a couple large windows, and the sun streamed in. The large live oak that stood outside had lost most of its leaves, and the early morning light crept across the floor and signaled to Melody that it was time to get up. She was still tired, but was it any wonder? Her sleep was a mass of visions of Farr Cottage, Arthur, and Alfred.

She tried burrowing deeper into the bed, but it was no use. Her body clock was still on Greenwich Mean Time, and it would take a few days to readjust. She only hoped it wouldn't take as long to put her dreams and sleep back in order.

In the kitchen she opened some of the items she had brought with her from Schiphol and the cream Gina had stopped to get at the market on the way home. Houston was blessed with some 24/7 supermarkets, and coming in as late as she had, it made it easy to get a few things to tide her over until she could do a thorough grocery run.

Coffee in her own mug in her own kitchen was the best! Melody had missed it so much and mornings with her mother flooded her memory. A tear came to her eye as she thought about her recent loss, but it was cut short by the ringing of the house phone.

Melody set her cup down and looked at the caller ID before answering. It showed "Chadwick Holdings" and listed the time as 8:01 a.m. She chuckled. Of all the people she had expected she might hear from on her first morning back, it had to be Pinky. She answered the phone.

Mr. L.T. (Pinky) Chadwick's secretary Marsha was calling. "Miss Farr? Mr. Chadwick is in meetings most of the day but would like to know if you can see him at four this afternoon. He will send a car for you and would like to take you to dinner. Can I tell him you'll come?"

Melody thought about her day and decided dinner with LT would be a treat. "Yes, I'll be ready. Thank you for calling." Melody hung up and took her coffee with her to her bedroom.

Showered, dressed, and ready for some breakfast, Melody went back to the kitchen. Her mother had been another one of the family who had done no more than was necessary to keep the house up-to-date. The last time anyone had refurbished anything had been when her mother had redone Melody's bedroom. Melody couldn't remember if her father had had anything upgraded either beyond adding the pool.

The kitchen needed some new appliances, the sink had a large chip in the porcelain, and at least two of the cabinets' doors would not stay closed. It seemed like everything needed some kind of attention. She made a note to call Mr. Baldwin, the trustee at the bank, to see if he could make arrangements for the repairs.

Melody looked at her watch and since it wasn't yet nine, she called the Vicarage at the church. Mrs. Grey, the wife of Rev. Erick Grey, answered. "Melody, when did you get back?"

"Hi Lisa," Melody said. "Late last night. Gina picked me up and brought me home. How is everyone?"

Lisa Grey chuckled. "You can imagine! Erick is running just as hard as ever. We have the Thanksgiving dinner in two weeks and then Christmas will be coming, so everyone is working overtime to get everything done in time. Same as every year, and of course, it is the beginning of the church year. So with Advent services, it just puts a lot on him."

Melody said, "I think he needs to rely on the Deacon more, but then, that is up to him. When do you want to get together about Thanksgiving? I brought some stuff from the duty-free zone that will work just great for the dressing. I also had some stuff sent to the Vicarage via UPS that should be there sometime this morning."

Lisa laughed. "Don't you want to unpack before you start taking in extra work? Hmm, I have a ladies group this morning and we have services this evening. But lunch tomorrow might be good. Do you want to come here or meet someplace?"

Melody opened her calendar, "I think it would be better if we meet at the Salad Hut at about one thirty. I am so hungry for a good salad! You would think lettuce, tomato, cucumber, and dressing would be easy, but it just doesn't taste right in England. So let's do the Hut, OK?"

Lisa confirmed and said she needed to get her husband another cup of coffee. "See you then!"

Next, Melody called Mr. Baldwin, but found he was not in the office and wasn't expected to be in until the next Monday. Calls done, Melody put her cup in the sink and took a bottle of water from the fridge.

One of the things Melody had wanted to do, as she had told her cousin, was to come back to Houston to find some of the letters, photos, journals, and more that she was sure must be in the library. She knew it would take more than a few minutes, and she wanted to see how much was really there.

Melody's great-great-grandmother, Lucy, had been well educated and loved books. Between her and her husband, Richard, the Farr House library was extensive. When the hurricane came through and ruined the original house, Richard, Lucy, and the servants had spent hours packing up the books and sending them to a barn that was still standing, was dry, and on much higher ground.

The double doors that led to the library slid silently into the wall pockets as she approached the room. As the doors opened, the lights came on automatically. Her grandmother, who had arthritic hands, had asked to have the lights setup this way when she opened the doors. The same system had been installed in the dining room, sitting room, and family room. Through the years, several modifications had been made to the house to accommodate her grandmother, and the lights were a minor change. An elevator was installed in the 1960's. A shower large enough for a bath chair, and a hospital bed in her room had replaced the stylish Art Deco bed she and Melody's grandfather had purchased when they married in 1940.

The bookcases in this library were very different from the ones in the library in Farr Cottage. These, in the Houston house, were floor to ceiling with a library ladder on wheels that could be moved from one bookcase to another. The lower three feet of shelves on the north wall, opposite the windows had doors that could be locked to secure the contents. In one cabinet, she knew the coin and stamp collections of her grandfather had been stored in it and in another, was a small safe where some old legal documents were kept.

Melody looked at the other cabinets to see what was there. In one she found several photos, un-framed, that had been taken of her great-great-grandparents when they married and a very old photo of Richard Farr before he married. She had seen a similar one of him at Farr Cottage along with a letter he had written to his parents before his father died. He had wanted them to see he was in good health.

A box of letters to and from Richard Farr's mother and brothers were also with the photos.

A cabinet was devoted almost exclusively to correspondence from and to her great-great-grandmother, Lucy Farr. Her beautiful, neat penmanship flowed across the pages, and the number of letters showed she was a prolific letter writer.

However, none of the other storage cabinets in the library had anything Melody was searching for. The desk was the next place where she looked. The "partners" desk from the original bank had been put in Richard Farr's study. But the desk her father used in Farr bank before it was sold to the big bank had a prominent place in the center of the room and several wing-back chairs in green leather were grouped near it.

None of the desk drawers yielded anything more than what Melody had already found. She sat back in her father's old chair and could feel his presence. He had been a cigar smoker, and the faint smell of his fine tobacco mixed with the lemon oil used to polish his old desk gave her a comforting feeling.

As she sat in the chair, she tried to think about what other places would have family items for which she was looking. However, Melody's thoughts soon turned to her cousin, Arthur, and the reason for her search.

She could close her eyes and see him sitting silently at the desk next to her in the library of Farr Cottage. At first glance, she had thought he was in his late forties. However, a birthday cake baked by his housekeeper, Nedda, to celebrate his forty-second birthday in October, set her straight.

At six feet, something, he was still taller than her five-seven. Alfred and Arthur both had the same caramel-colored hair, but her cousin had much more gray in his. Alfred's eyes were icy blue where Arthur's were more of a dark baby blue. They each had the same lean but muscular build with no sign of widening girth.

Suddenly, Melody bolted upright, almost tipping the chair back. Without realizing it, she was not just thinking about her cousin and Alfred but actually comparing them. Now was not the time to do that!

A quick look at her watch told her there was a good hour before she needed to prepare for her meeting and dinner with Pinky. She still wanted to look for her grandparents' and great-grandparents' things.

As she left the library and slid the doors closed, the intercom at the front gate rang. She crossed the foyer and inquired as to who was requesting entrance. A quick check of the monitor showed it was Reverend and Mrs. Grey. She had not been expecting them.

"Melody," Lisa Grey said into the intercom, "the UPS man just brought your luggage and a couple of boxes. Erick and I are on our way to a meeting and thought we would drop them off."

Melody had pushed the code to open the gate as Lisa Grey was talking. "Oh, you didn't have to do that, I could have gotten them. Just come to the back."

The reverend and his wife came down the long driveway while Melody went to the back entrance near the kitchen. The mudroom had a trolley she could use to move the things from where they would be deposited. She would take the elevator up and wouldn't have to carry the pieces. Melody had packed heavy and she didn't want to lug them farther than necessary.

The clock on the mantelpiece in Melody's room registered five to four as she put the final touches on her attire. A suit-weight wool gabardine black dress with a matching jacket, her grandmother's "Jackie Kennedy" pearls, and in her purse, a diamond broach to wear as a pendent on the necklace would make the outfit dressier for the evening. A small clutch purse for her phone, ID, and house keys rounded out the ensemble.

Melody always wore heels when she went out, and so her normal five foot seven was then an easy five nine. Pinky was her father's age and had been one of his best friends. The light strawberry-blond hair that had given him his nickname had long since turned white, but Pinky was what she had called him as long as she could remember.

His given name was Lionel Tyrone Chadwick. His mother had been a film buff and named her son for her two favorite actors, Lionel Barrymore and Tyrone Power. The night, he was born his father had been stuck in an early season blizzard and so wasn't present for his birth at the ranch. Although he had not been at the naming his father insisted his son be called LT and not Lionel or Tyrone.

The front gate intercom buzzed and she checked the monitor to make sure it was the limousine that LT's office said would be sent for her. Melody put the small remote for the gate in her clutch, slid into the back seat of the car, and closed the gate as the driver pulled through and out onto the street.

The ride to the office building located in the Energy Corridor took almost a half hour. But her cell phone had her e-mail account, and she had wanted to text Gina about the meeting that morning. There was nothing new on the e-mail, and Gina did confirm two maybe three possible fabrics she might like.

The driver drove Melody into the underground parking of the Chadwick Building. A security guard opened the back door for Melody and pushed the button to call the elevator. The guard told her to use the button marked "*E*" for the executive level. As the door closed, Melody smiled at the instructions. She had been a frequent visitor in this building since it first opened.

LT's secretary, Marsha, was waiting for her when the elevator door opened. "Miss Farr, welcome back to Houston. Did you have a nice trip?" Melody nodded in the affirmative. Marsha's soft cultured drawl was smooth and easy on the ears. "LT is waiting for you." Marsha held LT's office door open and then silently closed it behind her.

LT's office was very familiar to Melody. He had been one of her father's best friends, and on several occasions, she had accompanied her dad to visit his buddy's office. She was also close friends with LT's son, Mike, and daughter, Sally.

Melody walked quickly across the room. "Pinky! I am so happy you called."

LT winced at the nickname but extended his arms to give her a bear-hug. At six feet six, he was a big man, and "bear" was appropriate. She knew he worked out every day, so he was not fat. And the thick hair that had been the source of his nickname had turned white. He was a handsome man. "Come here girl, it's good to have you back. Did you miss your old uncle?"

"LT, if you were my *real* uncle I wouldn't have been sent to England. Being home is sooo wonderful. You just don't know!" She relaxed in the familiar arms of this old family friend. "Sit down and let's talk," he said.

LT motioned to a leather chair in front of his oversized desk, and Melody sat. "Can I get you a drink? I know it's after five somewhere in the world." Without waiting for her to answer, he walked to a seemingly blank wall and opened a wooden panel to reveal a bar. "Do you want bourbon or are you still drinking that "Scottish wine" your dad always preferred?"

"I will have a scotch with just a splash of water, please. Bourbon was never something I could get used to drinking although it works fine in barbecue sauce." Melody knew her dad's friend prided himself on his fine grilling skills and the sauces he made, none of which contained bourbon.

"Speaking of which … well, on second thought, we'll talk about that later, but I'm doing some barbecue this Sunday. So come and bring friends. Mark will be there with his girl, and it will give you two a chance to catch up."

When they had both taken their first sip and settled in their chairs, it was time to get to the purpose of the meeting. LT loosened his tie, took another sip of his drink, and fiddled with a paper on his desk.

Melody could tell he had something to say, but whatever it was, it was making the man uncomfortable.

LT looked her in the eyes and began. "You know how much we all miss your mother. She was a fine lady, and if your dad hadn't swept her up, I had my eye on her. But once she was my best friend's wife, well, you don't poach on your buddy's property. When your dad passed, I was married to Celia, but I promised your mom and myself that I would always look after her. That includes looking after you."

After another sip of his drink, LT continued, "I sit on the board of directors of the bank which is your trustee. Baldwin takes care of the paperwork, but I'm the one who really looks after what is in your dad's trust for you. Now, I don't know if you understand what happened with your father's will, but I'm going to explain it to you."

Melody shrugged, "All I know is that by the terms of my father's will, as it passed through my mother's, I am the sole inheritor. However, there is this clause that says I can't inherit until I am either married to "an approved" person or reach the age of thirty. If, at the time of Mother's death, I had not done either of these things, I was to live under the guardianship of a Farr male relative who had reached the age of majority, which in this case is considered to be thirty years-old. Is that about the gist of it?" The last was said with some sarcasm, and Melody winced at the thought of Arthur and Alfred.

LT watched the girl as she spoke. He had known her all her life and except for the death of her father, had never seen her in anything other than a happy, smiling state. Something was up with her stay in England, and he needed to get to the bottom of it. But not before he had discussed and explained other, more important things.

LT got up to freshen his drink and took her glass too. "Yes, and this is what I think I need to explain. Your grandfather, your father's father, died just two days after he landed on Omaha Beach on June 6, 1944, on D-Day. At the time, your grandmother and your daddy were staying with her family up in Connecticut." LT returned with their drinks and took his seat.

He continued. "They had gone to stay there when your granddaddy was shipped out and knew, since he was in the European Theatre of operations, he would be returning to the East Coast. Well, when word came, Charles Arthur Farr had been killed in action, your great-grandparents had your grandmother bring your daddy and come stay with them at Farr House. They redid Richard and Lucy's suite of rooms and turned one of the bedrooms near it into a nursery."

"Your grandmother Farr had a mother who was very strong-willed, and she didn't want her daughter and only grandchild going off to live in Texas. She wanted them to stay there but at the time, couldn't help raise your daddy."

Melody nodded. She had heard some of this story from her mother, but didn't interrupt LT.

He continued his story. "Your grandmother, as the wife of Charles Farr, inherited his estate. But he really didn't have much other than his death benefit from the army, his car, and what he had in the bank. His daddy hadn't given him anything and his granddaddy, Richard, hadn't willed anything to anyone except his son, Avery, your grandfather's father. Annis, who was Avery's sister, had gotten an ample dowry when she married, but when Annis and her husband Chester Lowell died in that air crash, Chester's father, Joseph Lowell, refused any Farr money and sent the dowry back."

LT shifted in his chair. "No, your grandmother really inherited very little. What Avery did do was give her a very generous allowance once a year. She and your daddy lived in the house so there was no expense there. Any major purchases, like a car, school fees for your daddy, or things like that were paid by Avery, and then later, your father used the allowance to take care of his mother. The money she was given was more like pin money. She used it for buying clothes for her or your dad, donations to the church or other charities, and books. She loved books and added quite a few to that library of which your dad was always so proud.

"When your gran passed, she had saved quite a bit of the pin money she had been given, and that is the money you and your mother got from her. However, the rest of the estate, the "Farr money", passed directly to your father when old Avery died. Your dad was very young but Avery's will had the clause about the "30 year-old" qualification.

"While your grandmother was the one to raise your father, it was the trustees who saw to his training in the bank and family trust. Your grandmother and your mother were not Farrs so by the wills of both your great-grandfather, Avery, and your father, they could not inherit."

LT took a drink from his whiskey. "I was with your father when they read your gran's will. Afterwards, we talked about the fact that he needed to make sure his own will protected your interests. You are a Farr, and the Farr money needed to come to you. I thought the world of your mother, and at the time, your dad was probably going to outlive me. But if something did happen to him and your mother were to remarry, she just couldn't take that Farr money with her to a new husband."

"The day he signed his new will, I was with him and he made me promise I would look after you and your mother. I tried to laugh it off, but he was dead serious. As it turned out, that promise came due before any of us wanted."

Melody sighed at the thought of her father in those last months and was still sad when his death was discussed. Looking closely at LT, she could see he was still affected by the loss of his lifelong friend.

LT looked at Melody. "You know, he was on the way to play golf with me when it happened. I had called the house to let him know I would be a little late getting to the club, but your mother told me he had already left. This was before the wide use of cell phones, and there was no way to call him. When I talked to the pro-shop at the country club to tell Charley that I would be along shortly, they said he hadn't arrived yet, but they would pass on the message."

"When I got to the club, he wasn't there and hadn't arrived, and I simply left. When I called Farr House, your mom said he hadn't returned home and didn't know where he could be. That's when I decided to drive the route he would have taken to see if maybe that old college car of his had broken down."

Melody remembered her dad's "college car." His mother had given the 1965 Ford Shelby Mustang to her dad when he graduated from college. The car was still in the garage at Farr House and Tommy Hernandez, the co-owner of the shop that serviced all the Farr family cars, had been after her to sell it to him ever since the death of her mother.

LT smiled at the thought of that car. Richard only drove it on weekends when he was going out by himself or with little Melody. It was in mint condition, taken care of religiously, and worth a small fortune. Nevertheless, he had to go on and finish his story.

"I drove from the country club golf course to Farr House and didn't see him. When I used the intercom at the gate to see if he had gotten back, your mother said he hadn't. Then I drove it again. That's when I saw the car sitting in the parking lot of a restaurant that was closed. When I pulled up to the car, I could see your dad sitting there, his head resting against the window, and the engine idling. I knocked on the window, but he didn't respond. The car door was locked. There was a store across the street, and I went there and called 911."

"There was a fire-station just down the road and they were there within minutes. One of the men used a tool to open the door, and the EMT guy caught him. He was dead, but they took him to the hospital anyway. It was later confirmed he had suffered an aneurysm. He must have just gotten the car off the road, put it in park, but didn't have time to turn off the engine before he died. I had to go to Farr House to tell your mother."

Melody remembered that day so vividly. She was in her room with the daughter of a friend of her mother, Lisa Harris. She was playing with Lisa while their mothers worked on something for the church. She didn't remember Pinky visiting, just the sound of her mother screaming. Melody was so scared that day.

"Telling your mother was one of the hardest things I had ever done. She just kept shaking her head and screaming. That's when I gave her the brandy." LT motioned to Melody. "You came in and looked so scared and alone. Jane Harris, Lisa's mother, stayed with your mom until some of the other ladies from the church could get there. Celia, my wife, came to arrange the food donations for the house."

The house was filled with people from the day her father died until after his wake four days later. Her mother was never left alone, and she stayed with her mom almost the whole time. Except for when she slept, they couldn't be separated. It was so different when her mother died; almost no one outside of the ladies at the church even called to give their condolences.

LT started to reach for Melody's glass on the way to the bar, but she shook her head. "I could do with some water, if you please."

He took the glass and got them both bottles of water. It was time to go on.

"Your grandmother Fitzhugh came from Boston, but she upset your mother so much I very soon took her to the airport and put her on the plane. But that's another story. Anyway, the attorney who made your father's will had explained it to your mother when we went to sign it, so she knew what was going to happen. You were too young to be at the reading of the will, and I guess your mother never told you what was in it."

"Now, you still have a year and some before you can inherit unless you get married, so what to do until then? Are your plans to go back and stay with your cousin in England at Farr Cottage or to stay here? If you stay here, well, as you can see, there are things we need to discuss." LT sat back in his chair and took a long swig from the bottle of water.

It was Melody's turn to fidget. What did she want to do? She still hadn't processed that last meeting with her cousin Arthur, and, how did she feel about Alfred? It was impossible to think about these things on command. She needed some quiet time to herself where the tension was gone and her mind could deal with the various emotions.

LT watched the girl struggle with her feelings. One of his wives, Margaret or Linda maybe, was like that. He decided it would be best just to press on and give her some of his bits of insight or outlooks on the matters they were discussing.

"When your mother died and we had to fulfill the terms of the will, the trustees asked a firm that handled confidential inquires to find your living Farr relatives. Lord Arthur Roland Farr, Viscount of Gibbons is not just the closest, but except for an unproven connection to a line of, oh let me see what that name was," LT shuffled some papers in a file, "yes, here it is. A Lord Alfred Oswin claims they are cousins in some way, but DNA has never been taken which could prove the association. What the report said was Lord Arthur is your only living Farr relative. True, there are some very distant cousins but they would have been distant even in old Richard Farr's time before he came to America."

LT chuckled. "Do you know that a Farr fought on each side in the Revolutionary War? Yep, one of those distant cousins, issue of a marriage between a great-great-aunt of Richard's, fought with the Americans. And the main Farr branch had an officer in the forces that fought for King George III on the English side."

"As I remember, this cousin of yours, Arthur, is forty-two, right?" LT wanted to get some feedback from Melody, and he guessed it would only come from some direct questions.

Melody shook her head in the affirmative. "We celebrated his birthday just recently. Actually, I thought he was older. But Nedda, his housekeeper, said forty-two, and I guess she is right." Melody sensed where Pinky was leading her, and she didn't want to go there. She needed time, and sitting in LT's office talking over a bottle of water and scotch was not what was called for.

"Look, LT. Right now, things are just a bit confusing, and although I would like to discuss all of this, it really needs more thought and contemplation than I have done in the last couple of days. Give me a chance to work it out in my mind, tackle my jetlag, and work the problem. I will be happy to discuss all of this with you. However, can I at least put you off for a couple of days?"

LT decided to change tack; he put his empty bottle in the trashcan under his desk and stood to get his jacket. "Look, I'm getting hungry. I didn't have lunch today, and I'll bet you didn't either.

So let's go get some food." Unobtrusively, he pushed a hidden button under the top of his desk which summoned his secretary.

Marsha quietly opened the doors to LT's office and waited for instructions. He told her to call down to the garage and tell them LT and his guest were ready to leave for dinner. She left as Melody slipped into the private bathroom behind one of the hidden doors near the bar.

LT and Melody came out of the elevator as the limo pulled to a stop. The driver got out and opened the door for Melody, and LT slid in beside her. As they pulled out of the garage and into traffic, LT pulled the mini TV down and switched on the evening news.

Chadwick Holdings was a family-owned global concern. Most of the people who traveled in their circle of friends who had red hair, green eyes, and a proliferation of freckles probably had some Chadwick, Harris, Lopez, or Higgins blood. The families had married among themselves, and their distinctive coloring marked them as part of the clan. From the ranches, oil fields, hospitals, and anywhere in between, every family member had a stake in the holdings, but it was LT who had been selected to run the company for the family. LT had been at the helm as long as Melody could remember.

Chadwick Holdings had done well for everyone, and LT was a well-known figure around Houston, the state of Texas, and even in New York and Washington. His ex-wives may not have been able to live with him, but his bevy of lovely ladies was the envy of many other men in his position and even re-married, never failed to call him a friend.

Melody and LT watched the top news stories and then Pinky switched the channel to a roundup of the day's business and markets. Melody turned her attention to the passing scenery.

Melody had been away from Houston for only a few months, but in that time, several things had changed. She was always amazed at how fast things were accomplished, and it was one of the differences she could see between America, Houston in particular, and England.

Almost the entire time she was in England, people were trying to impress upon her the age and longevity of everything around her. The heart of Farr Cottage was a stone house which dated back to the days of the Anglo-Saxons. Some of the buildings in the village had thatched roofs that had basecoats of thatch that were almost five hundred years old.

The village church, where so many Farrs had been vicars, was a substantial structure that dated to before the Conquest. Birth and death records, too, attested its great age. Families in the county, both high and low born, could trace family lineage through several hundred years.

Her own family; the Farrs, were Anglo/Saxons who had prided themselves on never bowing down to the Conqueror or his Normans. Her cousin, Arthur, had shown her the family tree, and the work she had done on the family history filled in just a small portion of the grand scale and scope of the history of England and the Farr's place within its majesty.

Melody shook her head. Arthur entered her thoughts, but she wasn't sure if she wanted to deal with him at the moment. She looked at the familiar landmarks along the way and how slowly the car was moving. She determined it would be a good half-hour or so before they got to the place where they would be eating.

Finally, Melody gave in to her thoughts of Arthur.

She hadn't expected to see him before she left, but as soon as Alfred had reluctantly left following their lunch, Arthur had arrived. John had driven to the station to fetch him from the train while she had been having her last encounter with Alfred in the Cottage's dining room.

She had gone back to her room to finish packing her carryon and getting her laptop stowed for the trip when she heard her cousin calling her name. Melody took her time getting everything in hand before leaving the room she had lived in the last few months.

By the time she walked down the main staircase, her cousin had removed his coat and hat. Arthur smiled as she walked toward him, but she could also tell he was not happy. When he asked her to join him in the library, she put her things on the table and followed.

"Melody, I am so relieved I have this chance to see you before you leave. John tells me that Alfred has been to visit and, uh, well, you know how I feel about him. I hope your trip back to your home will give you a chance to think about your position here at Farr Cottage. Oh, I know Alfred is closer to your age and more outgoing and all, but your future is too important to waste on someone who doesn't stand on a solid foundation." Arthur looked uncomfortable and the fine sheen of perspiration on his forehead was an indication of just how far out of his emotional safe zone he had traveled. For someone who had never shown any feelings toward her, he was trying hard not to trip on his emotions.

Arthur fumbled in his pocket for a handkerchief and wiped his brow. He just couldn't read the girl, and it un-nerved him. All the months they had sat side by side in this very same library working on their projects, he had found her to be a wonderful companion. Oh, at first, she talked too much when it was to both their benefits to keep questions to a minimum, but once that had been dealt with she had worked well with him.

Blindly, he knew he had to press ahead. "Melody, my dear, I *am* going to miss you. In these few months I believe we have become very comfortable with each other. Now, I don't mind telling you that the dinner party at Alfred's was a bit of an eye-opener for me. Uh, well, I really saw you as a very fine young lady and someone whom I had grown quite fond. I would even say I have a great affection for you and would like to pursue a relationship with you."

Melody had just heard Alfred pronounce his interest in her and now her cousin was doing the same. She had never thought of either man in that way, but now that the subject had been opened, it was difficult to put the specter of their declarations back in the bottle. She hadn't promoted the idea, or at least she was fairly sure she hadn't. For a few seconds, Melody looked back over her behavior and could not find fault with her demeanor.

Arthur watched her eyes, and being unfamiliar with the ways of women in general and Melody in particular, he was unable to determine how well his declaration of affection was being received. Like others in the same position, he figured more was better and pressed ahead.

He took her hands in his. "Melody, while you are visiting your home and friends in Houston, I would ask you to please think about what I have said. I think we not only work well together but would be a good fit as a couple. Please look on my proposal favorably, and if you need some extra time to make a decision, please take it. Just let me know if you will be longer than we had discussed." He brushed her cheek with a kiss and dropped her hands.

"Now, I will have John take you to the station so you can catch your train. Oh, and I applaud your decision to leave earlier than I had planned. Alfred doesn't need to be hanging about, and if you are not in residence, well, then he has no reason to be here."

Melody suddenly realized Pinky was asking her something. She looked over at him. "Sorry, I was thinking about something. I apologize, but I didn't hear the question."

LT laughed, "That's okay. I was asking if you were ready for Thanksgiving and Christmas yet."

Melody was happy to bring her mind back to the present. She noticed LT had turned off the news show and was sitting in a more relaxed manner. "I have some of the things ready, but as for the decorations for Christmas, I am still trying to find someone who'd put them up. The people Mother always got are fully booked and Gina is trying to find a group of students from the Design Institute who are doing that this year. She thinks they may have time to decorate the house."

LT patted her hand. "Don't worry. I think I have the solution for that, but we will talk about it over dinner. Are you hungry?"

Melody hadn't really thought about food since breakfast and realized she was very hungry. But also knew the place where they were eating had first-class fare in Texas-sized quantities. Yep, she was hungry and nodded. "I just hope they have great steak tonight. It's been awhile since I've had a good one."

The limo pulled under the marquee of a private club. The doorman opened the car door and tipped his hat to LT. The discreet plaque on the side of the door read, "St. Charles Club, Members Only."

The club also had several small dining rooms that seated anywhere from a cozy twosome to as many as twenty quite comfortably. The public areas that occupied three floors were built in an open design that allowed members the ability to see and be seen by the other members. The fee to join was more than $25,000 and then a yearly fee of $10,000 was due each January 1st. Money was never used at the club. Members paid their food and drink bills no later than the end of each month. No one was allowed to keep their membership if they failed to pay their tab on time. The membership list was limited, and those wishing to join numbered in the hundreds.

The manager of the club, as always, was dressed in formal wear and greeted them with a grin. "Good evening, Mr. LT, Miss Melody. It's good to see you have returned to us. I was so sorry to hear about your mother. She will be missed." The man guided them to the dining room and the maître d' took them from there.

Although the membership was limited to men, Melody's father had been one of the club's founders. When he died, the other members voted to keep her father's membership available for anyone acceptable to them whom Melody's mother might have married or to Melody's future husband, if he passed muster with the members.

The dining room was just as she had remembered it. Before the waiter had taken their orders, the chef came to greet Melody and LT. He then recommended a special dish to go with their steaks, and LT gave the nod for both the steaks and the vegetables. Next, the wine steward brought a bottle of LT's favorite and poured a sample for LT to try before filling each of their glasses.

Melody could almost see the tensions of the day slip away from LT as he savored his glass of wine. Running such a large concern was not easy, and he had been doing it for several years. Pinky had been at university with her father, and before that, he had attended the school at St. John's and then the Anglican High School for Boys. LT had gotten his nickname from his big brother, George, and the name Pinky had followed him all his life. Few people called him by his nickname anymore, but those who did, did so out of affection or fond memory.

LT set down his glass and turned his attention to his dinner guest. "Melody, when your mother died, I was in the house at her wake. Several items need attention. I think the kitchen should have some serious work done, and I know there are other things that should be addressed. Also, as your father's executor, I do not want you living in that house by yourself."

Melody was shocked. "But, why can't I live there? It's my home! I've lived there all my life and now you tell me I can't? Explain, please!"

LT reached out and patted Melody's hand. "Calm down. You have it all wrong. When I say "by yourself," I mean you should live there, but someone needs to be there with you. That house needs the care of a staff, and they will look after you. Your great-great-grand-father and his son built that house to be run with a cook, servants, and maids. Your grandmother understood. But your mother, bless her heart, tried to do it on her own."

Melody sighed and smiled. "Oh, if that is what you mean, whew, you had me worried I didn't have a place to live! But I can't pay a staff from my stipend."

LT laughed. "Just like your mother! The estate was setup to pay those expenses and no, it won't come out of your allowance. Your mother never wanted the estate to pay for more than the bare minimum. She was conserving your inheritance. I think she never understood just how much your trust was or what it was allowed to do for you."

"So tell me, where do I even look for people to work in the house? I have a girl who used to work for us a couple days a week, but she isn't available right now. Any ideas about where to start?"

The waiter came with the appetizer of game pâté, a special of the chefs. He refilled the wine glasses and then silently left LT and Melody to their conversation.

"Melody, I have just what you are looking for and the very people I would recommend. You remember Shirley? Well, it seems she wants to join my ex-wives' club. For the life of me, I'm a lovable guy. I just can't imagine why I can't keep a wife for more than a few years. Anyway, she left me."

Melody tried to remember the latest wife of her dad's friend, but couldn't really make the connection. "I'm sorry to hear that. How are Mike and Sally taking it?"

LT sighed; his son and daughter had never really warmed up to his last wife, so they were happy about the breakup. For him, he was coming to the realization it had probably been a bad idea to marry someone so much younger to begin with. Shirley was more than twenty years his junior. Perhaps it really was for the best, but this was not about him, He needed to get back to the business at hand.

"Thank you for your concern, but I need to help you get settled. Now, because Shirley is gone, I don't need the house we built. God that thing is … is … well, I'm sorry, but I should never have given her design OK on the plans. It looks like a collection of old outhouses to me, but I guess I'm just not into modern design. What it does mean is; the house is on the market, and I am moving into my penthouse in the Chadwick Building."

"Because I'm moving, my staff, even though they have been with me for several years, will not be going. Oh, I guess I could take Bellamy. But his wife, Mrs. Bellamy, is the cook, and I just don't have the need for a full staff in the apartment. What I want to do is send my staff, the whole bunch, over to Farr House. Bellamy and his wife plus the two sisters, Glenda and Pauline. The girls have been maids in the house for the last, oh, ten plus years. You won't be alone, and the house will be taken care of and protected."

Melody was surprised. Having so many people in the house so suddenly, well, that would take some getting used to. She started to question LT, but he held up his hand to stop her.

"I also want you protected. You are a young lady of means, and being on your own is not safe. Bellamy is a former special operations officer, and he's well versed in weapons of all kinds. He is also armed at all times and can protect you and the house. I know that the Hernandez family has always kept the cars in good running condition, but I would like it if you started using your grandmother's car. Bellamy makes a fine driver, and he would be with you when you go out. If your grandmother's car is not to your liking, I can have a proper car sent to you."

LT went on. "This is a lot to take in, but it's for your own welfare. I would hate for something to happen to you. Besides, then you won't have to find anyone to put up Christmas decorations, you'll already have your own staff to do it." He grinned at that last comment, hoping it would soften his proposal.

Melody just had to break in. "And what will this staff do when I return to England? Will they just stay in the house and look after it while I mark the days until my "majority" is attained? I just don't know about this. Four people. Isn't that a bit much?"

"Melody, when you get home tonight, I want you to walk around your house and look at how much work there is in just taking care of the main floor rooms. Then think about the rest of the house and what needs to be done there. You will see I am right."

LT sat back in his chair as the waiter removed the appetizer plates and began placing their main courses before them. The steaks were still sizzling, and the special vegetable dish the chef had told them about looked delicious. A different wine was sampled and poured before the waiters retreated so LT and Melody could continue their conversation over their food.

The interlude gave Melody a chance to think about what LT was telling her. She had several questions and took the lead when the waiter left. "Is all of this protection really necessary? I mean, who would want to harm me and why? I'm not a public figure or important to anyone beyond my own circle of friends. Really, I'm just an out of work historian with this "majority" issue hanging over my head."

LT jumped back into the discussion. "First off, you are very important. I guess some time I need to sit down with you and go over your father's estate in detail. Maybe then, you'll get some understanding of the extent of your worth. Moreover, anybody who knows even part of it would find you a good target for kidnapping or extortion." LT paused. "Melody, I take my position as your father's friend very seriously and, well, just believe me when I tell you this is for the best."

Melody put her fork down. "LT, ever since my mother died I have been told what is "best" for me. First that lawyer, Mr. Lynch, who came to deliver the will and stuff from Cousin Arthur, then Mr. Baldwin at the bank, not to mention Arthur, and now you. I'll be twenty-nine in a few months, when do I get to be my own person?"

LT took her hand. "Melody, I have known you since you were born. My wife, Celia and I, were your godparents when you were baptized at St. John's. Can you forgive me for trying to protect you? I know you are all grown up and you can walk away from any of this at any time, but all of us, including your cousin in England, only want the best for you. You are the last of old Richard Farr's line. Are you going to let it end here?"

Melody still didn't like it. She took her hand back and placed it in her lap. People were just trying too hard to manage her life. "Can I think about it?"

LT smiled and took a sip of his wine. "Sure, but please let me know by tomorrow."

The waiter took the dishes and the chef came to inquire about the food. LT praised him and commented about the wonderful taste of the vegetable the chef had recommended. The waiter put coffee cups on the table, and the wine steward brought them brandy from the bar.

Before LT could continue trying to convince her of anything, she asked about his children, Mike and Sally. Mike was her age, and Sally just a couple of years younger. Like most of the people she knew, they had all gone to St. John's for their grade schooling.

In years past, only the boys would have gone to the Anglican high school. But it had become co-ed in the seventies and it was where all of them had gone. It was a lot like the group of people Alfred had introduced her to in London at his dinner party.

LT beamed as a proud father should. "Mike has been accepted into the residency program he wanted at Massachusetts General, and Sally is about to finish her degree to become a teacher. There is a community of nuns in Indiana she is going to join when she finishes." LT frowned at the thought of his daughter becoming a nun, but he put that down to her "egg-donor" mother.

LT's first wife, Celia, was a wonderful woman, but she was more interested in her church than she was in her husband or children. She had been a very devout Catholic when he married her, and that had been one of her charms. A few years into the marriage, her ideas on sex and procreation were too much for LT, and they began to drift apart. She took to the confessional and LT to his work.

It wasn't that Celia had ignored the children, she didn't, but her interest in them was that they attend Mass with her at least two or three times a week. Her dream was for Mike to become a priest and Sally a nun. Nothing outside of the children's connection to the church interested her. Eventually, she asked LT for a divorce and the Church for an annulment based on her incompatibility with her husband's denial of her desire to have more children.

The Archbishop of Galveston looked at her case and granted her her wish. Within six months, she had married again and proceeded to fulfill her maternal destiny. Seven children in nine years seemed to make her happy. However, the last time LT saw her, it was at their son's graduation from medical school, and she was again pregnant.

LT needed to get back to the subject of Melody. They had both finished their brandy and coffee. LT signed the tab, and he held the chair as Melody stood to leave.

The limo was waiting for them under the marquee to the club when they exited. Without saying a word to the driver, they headed toward Farr House. As the car moved along the tree-lined winding street, Melody remembered the narrative she had written from her great-great-grandfather's accounts of his life in early Houston. In Richard Farr's day, Farr House and his estate had been located almost three miles past the last city dwelling. Now, the edge of River Oaks, where the estate was located, was engulfed in Houston and the metropolitan area which extends almost to Katy, Texas. The Houston metro-plex makes up the third largest city in the country.

The car turned into the drive, and Melody used the remote she always carried in her purse to open the gate. After the car passed through, she turned to look and make sure the gate closed behind them. The lights at the entry of the house came on as they approached.

The driver stayed in the car and LT opened the door on Melody's side. LT then waited until she had unlocked the Farr House door and gone inside. She had promised to call him the next morning.

LT settled back into the soft leather seat of the limo. His driver knew where they would be going next so he didn't take much notice of their route. Melody reminded him so much of her mother at that age. Of course, when Evie, her mother, was that age, she had just agreed to marry Charles, his best friend. LT always wondered what his life would have been like if he had become her husband.

If Melody was even ten years his junior, he wouldn't hesitate to court her. But she was his god-daughter and for him the operative word was "daughter." Sally would never get married if she followed her mother's dream and became a nun, but he would probably have the honor of walking Melody down the aisle when she married. He would make sure her wedding was the biggest and best Texas had seen in the last ten years or would see in the next ten.

The limo stopped at the door of his house. The rustic, reclaimed barn-wood it was sided with added to his perception of "collection of outhouses." He remembered the architect who designed the place. LT was sure there had been an added penalty for having to put his name on a design that looked like this. Shirley really did have bad taste. But they had just been married and he was still blinded by love/lust for her, so he gave her what she wanted.

The real estate agent who had listed the house the previous week had turned up her nose at it, but assured him it was just the kind of thing some of the under-thirty crowd would absolutely love. LT hoped that particular demographic would have the funds to pay the asking price. In any case, he would be moving over to the apartment after the weekend. One last barbecue was taking place after church on Sunday, and following that affair, he would visit other people for outdoor grilling.

Bellamy was waiting for him as he came in. He took off his hat and suit jacket and handed them over and then sat on one of the chairs near the front door so Bellamy could remove his boots. A pair of leather slippers was given to LT to wear, and he went off to his study.

Bellamy came in to ask if there was anything else he wanted. LT asked Bellamy to pour him a brandy and one for himself. "I need to talk to you about something."

"Bellamy, as you know, Mrs. Chadwick and I have parted ways, and this house will be on the market in a few days. After this weekend, I will have moved into the apartment and there won't be any reason for me to have as much staff in the apartment as I have now. Tonight, I talked to Melody Farr about you and Mrs. Bellamy as well as Glenda and Pauline possibly going over to her house to work. I told her you had been with me for quite some time now, and I recommended each one of you highly."

LT looked at his man-servant very seriously. "Miss Melody is all alone in that house, and she should not be left by herself. She should be protected and cared for. I can't think of a better place for all of you to go than to her house. If she consents, will you serve her as well and ably as you have assisted me? She is my god-daughter and is quite special."

Bellamy nodded to his employer. "Mrs. Bellamy and I have talked about what we would do. We had thought about taking a vacation. However, if we are needed elsewhere, we would help Miss Melody."

LT beamed. "Bellamy, I am pleased since we do need to care for Miss Melody. In terms of your vacations, though, she will be going to England in a couple or three months and when she does, she will be gone long enough for you and Mrs. Bellamy to take the time away that you wish. Then, when you two come back, the girls can have a couple weeks also. Now, all I have to do is get Melody to agree."

Melody looked around the kitchen the next morning and had to agree with Pinky that the place did need some work. As she drank her coffee, she took a short tour around the ground floor. She walked through the grand foyer her grandmother had loved so much, past the double staircases that led to the second floor, and then on beyond the doors to the library.

The ground floor had a small formal living room just to the right of the front door and on the left was the huge dining room. Beyond the dining room was a large butler's pantry, then the kitchen, and a mudroom that led out to the garage. On the left, past the library was an oversized, informal living room with French doors that opened to the pool deck, patios, outdoor kitchen, and cabana. The right side of the library had the study. A hallway led to the glass conservatory her great-grandmother had commissioned, and beyond which were the gardens and stables.

The house had a full second floor with fourteen bedrooms, a third floor with servants' quarters at one end, and the rest was attic space where furniture and family things were kept. Yes, LT was right; this house needed to be cared for.

Melody stood in the living room, looking out of the French doors at the pool. The pool likely hadn't been used for at least three years and needed work. Her mother had been in failing health and was afraid of letting Melody swim without anyone in the house to rescue her if she got into trouble. She would like to use the pool again as well as the outdoor kitchen.

The thoughts about the outdoor kitchen made her remember the barbecue at Pinky's on Sunday after church. Melody wanted to ask Gina to go with her, but she also needed to tell LT she would attend.

Melody reached for her cell phone and called LT. His private cell phone answered almost immediately. "Hi, Melody. Did you sleep well?"

She looked at her cell and grimaced that LT could sound so chipper after the amount of liquor he had consumed the night before. Melody hadn't tried to keep pace with him, but even she had imbibed too much. "I'm just fine. I wanted to tell you that you can count on me for the barbecue on Sunday and possibly Gina too. Also, uh, I think you are right about the house. If you get a minute sometime, stop by and we can look at it together."

Melody had expected LT to make an appointment for later that day or the next, but she heard him put his hand over the phone and tell the driver to stop at Farr House. "I am on my way. I hope there is some hot coffee when I arrive. See you in about ten minutes." The line clicked off.

Melody looked at her nightgown and hurried up the stairs to change. It was a good thing she had put a pot of coffee on when she got up.

Melody was dressed and ready to receive LT when the intercom at the gate rang just twenty-three minutes later. She opened the large doors to the house as he was getting out of the limo.

Together, they went back to the kitchen so he could get his coffee, and that is when he began his renovation project. After walking around the room opening and closing doors and drawers and then looking at appliances, he pulled out his cell phone and punched in a number. After half a beat, he had his construction supervisor on the line.

"Jose', good morning. I'm over at Farr House across from St. John's church. How far away are you?" LT listened for a moment and gave the man at the other end instructions to come to the gate, push the intercom and he would be let in.

LT and Melody continued the tour. Before they got half-way through the ground floor, the intercom buzzed. Melody let the man in, and LT went to the door to start the orders.

Jose' and his two brothers were the Chadwick Holdings' employees responsible for the physical properties of LT's house as well as those of his brothers and sister, and an old-maid aunt that still lived in the old Harris home near St. Luke's Hospital. Hugo and Jesus, Jose's brothers, were decedents of the family who had lived at the original Chadwick Ranch. Some of their cousins still lived on the ranch, but this part of the family had come with Elbeth Chadwick when she had married Dr. John Harris in the late 1800s.

Jose', Hugo, and Jesus all had college degrees from Texas A&M in construction management. Although they could have worked anywhere for anybody, they all preferred working for LT and Chadwick Holdings. Once a year the Chadwick, Harris,

Higgins, and Lopez families had a big three-day picnic and family reunion at the original Chadwick Ranch in Round Top, Texas. The families were made up of intermingled people who all had common roots and common ancestors.

Jose' took some photos, typed copious notes on the laptop he had with him, and followed LT and Miss Melody as they went through the house. In almost every room, there was some item in need of repair or replacement. They didn't discuss faded wallpaper or paint; that was a job for an interior designer. However, if the wall was damaged, a floor tile cracked, pieces of parquet flooring in need repair, or appliances due for replacement, it all went into his notes.

More than two hours later, Melody was ready to concede to the fact that a staff would be of use in taking care of the house. She had half agreed at the pool before LT arrived, but with everything they had found since then, it was obvious. LT would be sending them on Monday.

LT needed to get to his office to take an important call from someone in Asia. Jose' stayed on the task at hand, and Melody left to have lunch at the Salad Hut with Lisa Grey, the vicar's wife.

Lunch with Lisa was always fun and interesting, but before they had finished, the first effects of jetlag were about to send Melody to sleep. She had just gotten back to her house, turned the alarm system on, and gotten to her room when she found she could no longer keep her eyes open. Friends had told her it was worse when you went from east to west, and now she was inclined to believe them.

A little more than two hours later, she was awake. The phone by her bed was ringing. Not the house phone, but the cell phone she had used while in England. The caller ID said it was Alfred.

"Melody, hello? Hi, how are you?" Alfred's voice brought memories of his handsome face to her. For the first time in a couple of days, she found herself missing him.

Melody tried to shake the sleep out of her voice, but she was still groggy. "Hi. Oh, Alfred, I'm fine, just taking a little nap. It seems the jet lag has gotten me. And you, are you all right?"

"Very good now that I know you are OK. I was hoping to hear from you before now. Was your trip good?"

Melody really did want to talk to Alfred, but she was just so tired. "It was good. Look, I am really tired, but what if we talk online later or in the morning? Give me a time and I'll be on, promise. Then I can tell you all about my trip and, well, and everything else."

Alfred wasn't certain if he liked the sound of that last part, but he didn't want to push her. "Sure, I'll be on at 9:00 a.m. your time in the morning. I want you to get a good night's sleep and tell me all about your trip and your news. You go back to sleep. Bye!"

The call finished and Melody was left holding the phone. She put it back on the nightstand, plugged the charger in, and covered herself with the comforter.

Melody and Gina had a date for brunch, and after more than twelve hours of sleep, Melody was finally rested. It was six when she woke up, and a wonderful shower got her started on the morning.

Everything they would need for the brunch was cut, sliced, diced, and ready in the fridge; she just had to put it together. Melody took a fresh cup of coffee and plugged her laptop into the outlet in the kitchen to wait for Alfred to come on-line.

At the appointed time, the familiar *ping* hit her inbox. She opened his message, and they started conversing with each other via instant message.

Melody told him all about her shopping spree in Schiphol Airport and the flight to Houston. He asked her about the friend that met her at the airport and if she had found everything in her home in order. She told him about Gina and the dinner with LT but not the substance of the meeting. She wanted to talk to Arthur before she said anything about her plans to return to England possibly being delayed.

There was an intercom in the kitchen for the front gate, and while she was still online, Gina buzzed to be let in. Melody entered the code and then told Alfred she had a guest who was about to arrive for brunch but would like to talk to him again later. They made a date for the afternoon.

Gina arrived at the front door just as Melody did. Gina was carrying some fresh croissants from the little French bakery down the street, and Melody gave her the champagne bottle to open to make the mimosas. An egg casserole was just about to come out of the oven, and Melody took a few minutes to finish a hollandaise sauce to go with the eggs and ham.

Gina pulled the three fabric swatches out of her bag and put them on the sideboard. In the sunlight of the kitchen, one of them didn't have as nice a color as she had thought, but it would be up to Melody to decide if it would work for her.

Eventually they were able to take their food, the mimosas, and refills of everything to the breakfast room. Her mother had loved this particular room with its windowed wall looking out over the lawn and to the cedars that lined the bayou.

Great-great-grandfather had planted the cedars along Buffalo Bayou before he had ever built the first house on the property. The hallmark aroma and oil of the cedar was a natural mosquito repellent, and it made sitting outside in the early spring and late fall much easier. Now, however, there was a mosquito repelling system in the misting sprayers that were all around the patio, pool, cabana, and outside kitchen area.

Melody and Gina spent several minutes catching up on their news. After the decision she had taken about the renovations on the house and agreeing about the need for some staff to help take care of the place, Melody was still not ready to say anything about it to her best friend. She had planned on calling her cousin after the barbecue on Sunday and letting him know she would be staying longer in Houston.

Gina felt Melody was quieter than usual. All the time Melody was in England, they had 'talked' via instant message almost every night, but writing something and hearing the inflections in the speaker's voice was a different matter. Gina had the suspicion something had happened in England that Melody was not telling her.

"Come on," Gina chided, "tell me what is going on. You've met someone, and I want all the details." Melody blushed. "See, I knew it! You have. Tell me! Tell me!"

Melody took a sip of her champagne cocktail. "There really isn't anything to tell. I've told you about Arthur and Alfred. They kind of, oh I guess you could say, agitate each other, but more like two kids fighting over the same toy. It's just that the last night we were in London Alfred gave a dinner party. The next day, I realized they're really going at each other, and I'm the reason."

Gina put more orange juice and champagne in each of the glasses, waiting for her friend to continue. "And?" she said.

Melody put down her fork, took another sip of her drink, and told her friend what had occurred. After she finished, she sat back and waited for her friend to react.

"Gee, hmm, not what you had expected. So, now these two guys are in England, you're here, and this trip is to let them cool off? I thought you had come back to see your home and friends."

The mock pout Gina affected was quite well-known among her friends. "Are you going to pick one or just throw them both back?"

"Gina!" Melody laughingly admonished, "They're not fish! I don't know. That's the problem. All this time, well, I never really thought about either of them like that. My cousin was my cousin, and Alfred was the neighbor who took me to church or dinner once in a while. Now, well, now I have caught myself comparing them, thinking about them, it's un-nerving."

"All I wanted to do was spend what time I had to in England, do whatever work my cousin wanted on the family genealogy, and come back here. I have just over a year before I reach the magical age of thirty, but they want to complicate everything." Melody took a croissant from the plate, tore it apart, and started munching.

"This afternoon, Alfred is supposed to IM me again. We talked yesterday afternoon, but I was so out of it with jet lag I couldn't hold any kind of intelligent conversation. We were on IM when you came this morning."

Gina asked Melody several more questions. "Is there any feeling there for either one? I know what you have said about them in the past, but it was more of a "He's this height, age, hair color, blue eyes, etc. …". I mean, you can get that off a driver's license. There has to be more."

Melody put up her hands in surrender. "Hey, I have nothing. I mean, they are nice guys and all that, but I just hadn't thought about either one of them as dating material. I do kind of miss them, but maybe that will change. Who knows?"

Melody stood and started removing the dishes from the table. Gina picked up several things and followed her into the kitchen. In a few minutes, everything was cleaned and put away.

Gina took the fabric swatches from the sideboard, and for the next few minutes, the two girls discussed the silk. A buzz from the intercom startled Melody.

Tommy Hernandez was at the front gate. He was coming to get one of the cars from the garage. Melody let him in.

Tommy's father and brothers owned a large auto service company in Spring Branch, an area in Houston not too distant from Farr House. The family had a long-term agreement with the Farr's to take care of the Farr family cars, and part of it was each of the cars currently stored in the garage would be driven at least once a month on a rotating basis. Tommy told her that today it was her mother's car.

Tommy was the third generation of the Hernandez family who owned the garage. His grandfather had started it after World War II when the GIs came back and wanted to buy cars. The automobile companies had not produced anything except military stock, so old used cars were the only thing available. An injury during the fighting had given the returning vet a couple hundred dollars. His job in the army, repairing and servicing anything from a tank to a general's car, gave him the experience and know-how to fix just about any kind of car available at the time.

Julio Hernandez rented an empty one-bay repair shop, bought some used tools, and opened for business. He and his wife Lucia prayed every night that he would have enough at the end of the day to buy food for their growing family. A notice in the paper about six months after he opened advertised army surplus engines and transmissions for sale. With the remainder of his money in his pocket and the prayers of his wife, he used the money to get five engines and two transmissions.

It made a huge difference in the success of his business. He and his brothers worked nights and weekends to refurbish the used equipment. Before the first piece was finished, he sold and promised to customers all he had bought. At the next auction, he and two of his brothers pooled their money and bought enough engines and transmissions to fill a large truck. Soon, he was looking for a surplus one-and-a-half ton truck with which to take their purchases home.

Melody went out to the front of the garage to talk with Tommy. "Hi! Haven't seen you in a long time, how's the family?"

Tommy smiled, "My little Layla is planning her Quinceañera, and she is going to bankrupt me! She wants one of those long white limousines to take her to the party. But I told her, she can't have one until she gets married, and that won't happen until she finishes college."

"And what happens if she brings some boy home before that, and he wants to take her away from you?" Melody chided him, "Then what will you do?"

Tommy laughed. "You know, the best protection for my daughters was the day they allowed open-carry in the State of Texas. No boys want anything to do with a girl whose father carries a gun!"

Melody laughed with him. She knew he was joking, but the boys didn't. "LT Chadwick has given me some advice about my grandmother's car, and I want to know what kind of shape it's in and what you think about it being put into use on a regular basis."

Tommy rubbed his chin, pulled the corner of his mustache, and thought for a few moments. "It is a beautiful car, mint condition. My family has taken care of it since long before she passed away, or at least my father did. It's in great shape, but if it were me, sell it and get a new one. The new models have better gas mileage, better protection on the front and back, and ride better. For its age, it is a good car, but it's time for it to go to a good home."

Tommy turned and pointed to the car of Melody's father. "Now *that* is the car you can sell me. I would love to drive Layla to her party in his car."

Melody laughed. "If I remember right, a proper Quinceañera dress wouldn't fit in Father's car." A vibration and loud tune from her pocket suddenly broke the conversation. Melody pulled out her ringing cell phone to look at the caller ID. With a standard "I have to take this," she walked toward the mudroom door and said, "Hello."

The caller was LT. "Hey, girl. How is your day going? I'm sending the staff over to your house for a walk through before they make the move on Monday. And Jose' is coming with a crew of men to do some painting in the servants' quarters."

Melody was surprised, "I thought the staff wasn't coming until Monday after they clean up the remains of your barbecue mess? When are they getting here?"

She could almost hear LT smiling through the phone. "Actually, we are already here, I'm at the gate, and they are right behind me. So open up!"

"OK, but come around to the garage. Tommy Hernandez is here, and we're talking about the cars. See you in a few minutes." Melody hung up the phone as she went through the kitchen to open the gate.

LT's car, two SUVs, and a pickup with five men in it descended on the garage area. The men in the pickup swarmed out and started pulling things out of the back of the truck. One of the SUVs had Jose' in it, and he started barking orders at the men as soon as he got out of his vehicle.

Bellamy drove the other SUV, a larger more expensive model than the obvious work vehicle of Jose'. Mrs. Bellamy and the two maids, Glenda and Pauline, got out and looked around. John Bellamy, retired Special Operations officer, extended his hand while LT introduced the group.

"This is John Bellamy. Just call him Bellamy. He's been to that fancy butler/house manager school in England, and they taught him he was only known by his last name. And this is his wife, Gilly Bellamy, the best cook/chef I've ever had plus the two sisters who prefer to be called Glen and Paul." LT finished the introduction and turned to Tommy.

"Can we talk about this car while they get to know each other?" Tommy and LT walked to the open garage door to discuss her grandmother's car. Gina, surprised at the crowd of people, mouthed the words "call me" and went back through to the kitchen to get her things.

Melody reentered the house to talk to the people who would probably be her new staff. Tommy came in before she started and said he would be in touch. LT joined the group for the walk through.

The first thing LT and Jose' wanted to know was what rooms would need to be painted for the staff quarters. Melody hadn't really thought about it before, but now, she was put in the position of deciding where they would stay.

There was a nice big apartment over the garage where the last chauffer and his wife had lived. When Melody's grandmother died, her father no longer needed a driver, so another family in the area employed the couple. There was also a large studio-type apartment on the other side of the kitchen where the last butler, Mobley, lived until he retired a few years before her grandmother passed away. Anytime they had had maids, they usually used any one of the four rooms on the third floor near the attics. The group looked at all of them and decided the girls would take the garage apartment and Bellamy and Mrs. Bellamy the studio near the kitchen.

"Miss," said Bellamy, "with the large butler's pantry, there is plenty of room for us. I grew up over a garage, and it is really unnecessary to repeat the experience."

Melody smiled. "You'll have to tell me more of your background sometime. I just hope you will all be happy here."

Jose' put his men to work, and the group continued the tour. LT did most of the talking and Melody just tagged along.

The closer it got to the time when she was supposed to IM with Alfred, the more worried she got that she would be late. "Pinky, I've got a previous engagement to talk to someone online. Can you do this with Bellamy and the rest? I would hate to be tardy. He is in England, and it will be late there. I don't want to keep him awake."

LT's 'father radar' caught the reference to a "he" in England. "So who is it, Arthur, Alfred, someone else?"

Melody looked at her shoes, "It's Alfred. We didn't really get a chance to talk since I've returned, and we made the appointment for this afternoon. Nothing special, just a chat."

LT nodded. He was going to have to have a long talk with this girl and very soon. Part of the reason he wanted to have a staff in the house with her was to help monitor who she was seeing. He worried she would fall victim to a smooth-tounged adventurer who was out to get her money, and he couldn't allow that. She just needed to be careful, and he had to make sure nobody harmed her.

Jose' walked ahead with the group while LT hung back. "Where will you be in case there are questions?"

Melody had her laptop in her arms and could take it any place in the house. "I'll be in Father's study." With that, she turned and left LT so he could rejoin the others.

The study was a favorite of all the Farr men. Originally designed by her great-great-grandfather, it was one of the few rooms still left of the original house. The oak paneling hid bookcases, a bar, and two large safes. Through the generations, there had been slight changes and moderations, but it was essentially the quiet retreat Richard Farr had designed it to be.

A few years ago, Melody had asked her mother to allow for some internet cable to be installed when the house had needed to be rewired. The men who came to do the work were able to convince them to have the wireless hubs installed that would make the integration of the lights, alarm, and security systems so much easier. The year before her mother passed away, Melody was able to upgrade the Wi-Fi to allow her to use the internet from any room.

Melody took a bottle of water from the mini-fridge under the credenza, one of the focal points of the room, behind the large partner's desk. The seating area had a comfortable sofa, two wing-back chairs, and some tables on which to set things. There was also a laptop table Melody had put in the room to do her homework. No sooner had she gotten set up, the familiar electronic "*ping*" told her Alfred was online.

For the next forty-five minutes, the two exchanged pleasantries about their recent activities. Melody told Alfred about the brunch she had just had with Gina, the barbecue LT was hosting the following day, and how much she was looking forward to church in the morning. Alfred reciprocated with a funny story about a dinner party he had attended at the home of one of the guests Melody had met during that ill-fated dinner party in Alfred's own London home.

"Beryl Somersby and her brother Nicky live not too far from me and I thought I could just walk over. But good-old London weather, you'd think I'd know better. Even with my brolly (umbrella), I was soaked before I got there. Nicky had me take off the wet things and put on his robe, but then Maude came in. You remember Maude Harbison? She took one look at me, and I thought she was going to kill Beryl. Nicky and I just quietly left the two of them to sort out their tempers. I still can't figure out what put the bees in their bonnets."

Melody chuckled as she read the story. A slight tap on the door brought her back to her surroundings. "Come in." She typed a note to Alfred to wait a moment and looked up to find LT in the doorway. She motioned for him to come in.

LT looked at the big desk where her father had spent so much time when he wasn't at the bank. "This room has a lot of good memories." He nodded his head toward the desk. "Anyway, everyone is busy doing whatever it is they do. When you're done, I need to speak to you."

Melody pointed at the computer. "Let me finish this up and we can talk." Her fingers flew over the keyboard as she told Alfred good-bye, and they set a time to speak again on IM. Closing the laptop, she turned her attention to LT.

LT settled into one of the chairs facing Melody. "Mrs. Bellamy has been going through the kitchen and taking an inventory of the equipment. Bellamy has also looked in the butler's pantry and china closets in the dining room and has taken a cursory catalog of what is and isn't available in the way of dishes, serving pieces, and whatnot. There are some things in the vault here," he pointed to one of the panels, "but mainly the major items are still at the bank in the big vault."

"Your great-grandmother was a shrewd woman. Her people all came from money so when they made it or more of it, they didn't feel the need to become big spenders. At the turn of the last century, when the first big oil strikes made some people in Beaumont and Houston so rich, well, that didn't apply to most of the newly minted millionaires. They would go to Europe, New York, or England and buy all kinds of things, but when they started to lose their new money, it meant they had some things to sell. That's when your great-grandmother was able to extend her china, silver, and jewelry collections."

Melody had never known about that but it did answer some of the questions she had always had about certain pieces of jewelry in the safe. She also remembered a Georgian tea and coffee service her grandmother had insisted the butler or maid use when they served her afternoon tea or when guests came. She hadn't seen it in years and had begun to think it was the kind of false memory children often have of events that occurred when they were too young to remember clearly.

Turning to LT, Melody blurted out. "You mean the bank has been the family's storage unit for fine things all these years?"

LT laughed. "Essentially, yes. When your father sold the family bank to the one that owns it now, that was part of the agreement. He didn't really have any place to keep it here when the silver wasn't being used. Also, he didn't want it as a magnet for thieves when he was away and just you and your mother were alone in the house. So the purchase contract has this extra side covenant that covers the silver, his gun collection, and jewelry boxes."

Melody thought she knew all of the secrets, but it was obvious she still didn't. "So now that the new staff has had a look at everything, what is their assessment? I mean, what is the verdict?"

LT went to the bar he knew was hidden behind the panel to the right of the big desk. He motioned to Melody to find out if she wanted a drink. He brought her a short scotch while he settled down with bourbon and then said, "Altogether, things are OK. Considering the number of years it's been since there was any staff in this house, the kitchen could use a few pots and pans, but especially, there is a lack of good items in the linen and china departments. All will be replenished. You will need to tell Bellamy what you want. It is up to you to actually make sure he knows how you want things done." LT took another sip of his drink. "Bellamy is a gem, so is his wife. But if you just 'live' here and don't take an active role in telling them what you want or like or even don't like, well, then you'll get what they think you want."

Melody sipped at her drink and thought about what LT had said. "I suppose so, but I guess what I have a problem with is having so many people in the house. I mean, you're used to it, but I'm not."

LT laughed. "Most of the time I don't even see the girls for days or even weeks at a time. All I know is the place is clean, my clothes are ready for me to put on, and there are always fresh towels in the bathroom. As for Bellamy and Mrs. Bellamy, she is a wonderful person who keeps me on my diet and doesn't let me get more than five pounds heavier than the doctor says is good for me."

LT went on, "Bellamy, well, he is quietly 'there' to do what needs to be done. It seems he always knows when I need a bourbon and branch or if a cup of coffee will fit the bill. Trust me, you'll get used to it in no time."

After another sip of his drink, he took up another subject. "There is only one weekend between now and Thanksgiving. I am going to New York, and I'm taking you with me. Bellamy and Mrs. Bellamy are going with us to do some shopping for your house and, well, I want them to impress some people I will have a meeting with there. I want you to do some shopping."

Before Melody could interrupt, LT continued. "The first Saturday in December is the last of the charity balls for this year. I have tickets, and you are going with me. You'll need one of those fancy ball gowns or whatnot, and since a lot of the ladies around here get their stuff from stores here or in Dallas, it might be nice to not walk in looking like three other gals. We'll only be gone for a couple of days, but since I don't think you have ever seen New York, it might be nice if you did."

Melody thought about a trip to just go shopping. She had never liked the activity anyway, but traveling somewhere to do it didn't make her bucket list. "If you let me take my dressmaker, Louisa, I'll go. We can see what's there, and she can make me something much better which will fit just me and not 20,000 other women."

LT nodded. He wanted Melody to get out and meet some eligible young Texas boys, maybe get some interest going there. He figured it was time to tackle the "English problem" as he had started to call it in his thoughts. However, before the conversation could get started, he wanted to square away the dinner arrangements.

"Melody, do you have any plans for dinner this evening or would you like to just get something to eat here?"

"No, no plans. I had the brunch with Gina late in the morning, but other than that, I didn't make any plans." Melody tried to think of what was in the house that might make up a dinner and started to get up to check the kitchen.

A little more forcefully than he intended, LT stopped her. "No, sit down. Let me get Bellamy in here and ask him to have Mrs. Bellamy check the kitchen for food. If there isn't any, it will either be bought or found someplace, but you are not to do it." LT softened his tone, "You need to let the staff do their job, and this is the first lesson."

LT pulled out his cell phone and called Bellamy. "Please come to the study, it's the room next to the library."

Within seconds, there was a soft knock on the door and Bellamy came silently into the room. "Yes, sir?"

LT gave him directions to find something to eat or go get what Mrs. Bellamy would need to make dinner. "We'll eat in the dining room. In the meantime, there is a bar behind that panel, and I would like a bourbon and branch and Melody wants a scotch with water but no ice."

LT winked at Melody as Bellamy moved about the room to make the drinks and serve them. Before Bellamy left the room, however, the conversation turned to England, and LT wanted Melody to understand that almost anything could be safely discussed in front of the servants. "I have wanted to ask you about the last few months in England, and I guess now is the time. Tell me about it."

Melody sipped her drink, thought about the request, and made some decisions before she began. She didn't tell LT about the first few days when Nedda, her cousin's housekeeper, had put her to sleep in the servants' quarters of Farr Cottage. She did tell him about meeting the vicar, his wife, and grandson. He asked her some questions about Farr Cottage.

She described the huge house that had been expanded over the years to reflect the style and size of the family at each time period. She told him about the portrait of the Farr family shown to her by her cousin. The one in the style of Dobson was of particular interest. "When I had asked him about the title, Viscount of Gibbons, he showed me the portrait of the family and the little dog the fleeing future Charles II's entourage had left at the Cottage. The history of the place and the family is quite interesting. Even if I wasn't a Farr, it is worth the study."

Melody put her drink down and continued. "The part of the family I worked on while I was in the Cottage was the story of Richard Farr and some of your ancestors. John 'Big Red' Chadwick, Elbeth, Doc Harris, Jeremy Higgins, they were all part of the Farr family narrative. Some of the things I want to get done while I am home will be to find pictures, journals, and letters, and anything else that might add to that part of my heritage or the continuing chronicle."

"My cousin sent me a photo with the letter I received from him initially, but it didn't serve him well. I thought he was much older from the picture, but it turns out he is only forty-two. He's well over six feet and although he is not athletic, he does have a lean, muscular build." Melody had run out of things to say about her cousin, but LT certainly wasn't interested in how he looked.

"Yes, yes, that's all fine, but what kind of man is he? What does he do for a living?"

Melody thought about what she would tell her godfather. "He's a quiet man. For the last few months, we sat at desks next to each other, and for hours, we quietly worked away on our separate projects. Actually, it was very peaceful in the Farr Cottage library, and we seemed to fit well together."

She took a sip of her drink and continued. "As far as what he does, well, he is what they call a "*book*." He has a photographic memory and while he was up at Oxford he …"

LT put his hand up, "Why do you say "up" at Oxford? Why not just say when he was in Oxford?"

Melody chuckled, "Hmm, I guess it's from geography. The Cottage is in Kent, and that is south of Oxford. So, if you want to get to Oxford, you have to go "up." Anyway, when he was *at* Oxford, a professor or tutor taught him how to catalogue the little bits of information he would acquire as he read. The way he was taught also lets Arthur find other little bits of information that go with the first."

LT looked at her. "But don't computers have all of that beat? He's outmoded. He makes a living doing this?"

Melody smiled at him. "Computers can't do anything we don't tell them to do. What Arthur does is go through his memory banks and find the information and the other threads that are attached to the first bit. Now, if he makes a living from it, I don't know. He is a consultant expert with several ministries. I'm sure they pay something, but he does have the estate which provides most of his living. One of the things he told me on more than one occasion was the Farr family has always been a loyal servant of their king, in this case queen, so it could be, well …"

Melody trailed off. She had wondered about his situation. A look at the Cottage and grounds would not denote there being a lot of money, but the family had been going for more than a thousand years, that is a long time to accumulate something.

LT watched the girl. While she talked about her cousin, she had not shown any special interest in him. Her eyes didn't light up, and there was no urgency to tell old LT all about this wonderful man. No, he didn't think this is where there was any problem.

"When are you supposed to return? Do I need to call your cousin and get him to extend your stay here?" LT wanted to see if this would get a rise out of her.

"I would like it if you talked to him. With all the things going on in the house, I don't really want to leave before it is finished." Melody sighed. "Do you think it will be finished before my birthday at the end of May? At least, then I would only have another year to go to get out from under the will."

LT's eyes flashed with a bit of anger. This was not the first time she had mentioned being "under the will" or some such verbiage. "Why are you so eager to get out from under the will? Is this life so difficult for you?"

Melody shook her head. "It's not that. I just don't like marking days. I want to get on with my life."

LT set his drink down and took her hand. "Come with me girl. Where is that old map of Houston your daddy used to have in this room?" He was looking around the room, but before he had scanned all the walls, Melody told him it was in the library.

"Mother moved it in there after Father died." LT marched her into the library, turned on the light, and pointed to a seat at the big desk.

"Sit," was all he said. He took the antique map from the wall and swept some papers aside on the desk. He put the framed, yellowed diagram on the desk in front of Melody.

The desk had two green-shaded desk lamps, and he took one to shine on the item he wanted her to see. He pointed to a red-shaded area that she recognized as the property where they were currently sitting. "This is Richard Farr's original purchase for this house. All of this is property your great- great-grandpa bought when he built the original house for his Lucy. This over here," pointing just south of the red patch, "is the land he gave for the church. Do you see anything else about this map? Any feature that might not look like other maps?"

Melody had seen this map for as long as she could remember. She had sat with her father in his office when she was a little girl, and he would show her where Farr House was. However she couldn't see anything special about the rest of the map. She told this to LT.

Surprised, LT pointed at the red coloring on the map. "This is where this house is, the church property is here, are there any other red patches on the map?"

Melody looked again. There were several red areas, some bigger than others and not all in the same part of Houston. "Well, sure, there are several red places. They aren't all the same color of red, and it looks like someone colored them in by hand. But, yes, I see them."

LT took the framed map and motioned for Melody to follow him back into the study. He propped the map up on the sofa, refilled their glasses, and sat across from Melody. "Girl, the red on that map is part of what your family has been building up so you could complain about "marking the days" until you're no longer under the will that protected all of this for you."

LT let what he said sink in while he savored his drink. Melody looked at the map more carefully this time. By following the roads, which had been marked on the map, she was able to see there were properties in several parts of the city; downtown, the area where the house was, a parcel where the medical center now stood, and a nice piece near Rice University. She didn't know what property prices were, but she knew all of this made quite a sizeable asset.

Melody had never thought about what she would inherit. She knew from what her mother had said to her that there was the money from the sale of the bank. Her father had also told her the stories about the discovery of oil on the land Richard Farr had taken in exchange for a loan to keep a ranch going during the drought in the late 1880s. The rancher from Beaumont, Tim Norton, had lived to see his land awash in oil, but sadly, the lean years had left him with poor health and a trainload of creditors. Richard Farr had done well from the $500 he gave for the thousand acres of land.

If LT's purpose behind this exercise was to teach Melody the extent of her inheritance, it was working. Sheepishly, she asked him to forgive her for acting so selfish. "Pinky, when you put it this way, whew, a year is nothing. Why didn't anyone ever tell me this? Something could have been said when my mother passed away."

LT ran his hands through his full head of hair. "Frankly, that was my call. Baldwin, the guy at the bank, had said it might be best for you to know something about the extent or at least part of it. However, what I have shown you is not everything, and I am certain your mother never knew even the half of it."

"I had just hoped you would go to England, stay until you were thirty, and then we could deal with it. I saw the picture of your cousin, the one he had sent with the letter. Well, he didn't look all that interesting to me. I figured you would live there. He seemed capable of looking after you. Then, when it was time, you could come home. When you left early, I thought maybe something had happened, so I guess the next question is why you are home?"

Melody laughed. "First off, I'm a Texas girl, and I was homesick for Tex-Mex, barbecue, and the Texans! I spent several months writing the narrative to the story of my ancestor, Richard Farr. It was about Texas, ranches, Houston, and the people he knew. I also want to celebrate Thanksgiving and Christmas in my own church. Is that so hard to understand?"

Shaking his head, LT joined her laughter. "Well said, girl. Anything else bring you back?"

The smile faded from Melody's face. Had things in England been so bad or was she overwhelmed with Arthur and Alfred? She had been thinking about it since she boarded the plane from Amsterdam. The long flight gave her an ample opportunity to examine her most recent past. Her conclusion was she had felt growing affection for both men, and it felt odd in some way.

LT watched as Melody hesitated to answer his question. Something was going on in her mind she might not be ready to talk about, but he felt he needed to know. If there was a problem, he had to recognize what it was if he was going to fix it or deal with it. Was it this cousin or maybe the other guy, Lord Alfred Oswin? Maybe it was time to do a more thorough check on both men.

Their attention, however was diverted when Bellamy came to announce dinner.

LT held Melody's chair and Bellamy served the food. Melody recognized some of the raw ingredients she had used for the brunch and realized Mrs. Bellamy had used them for a lighter-than-air omelet, fruit compote, asparagus in hollandaise, and for dessert, orange sherbet.

Melody looked up at Bellamy, "Please tell Mrs. Bellamy I like what she has done with the odds and ends that were left from brunch. This is super!"

Bellamy nodded, "Yes, miss, I'll tell her."

LT asked Bellamy if the painters had finished. Bellamy, ever so very efficient, gave LT a rundown of the progress. "The painters have finished their work, and Glenda and Pauline have cleaned both sets of quarters. There is a problem with one of the lavatories, and Jose' will be back tomorrow to repair it. Mrs. Bellamy has finished an inventory of the kitchen, Glenda had done one of the linen closets, and I have finished most of the rest of the house. I looked at the security system first, as you requested, and it was state of the art twenty-five years ago. Now, however, it needs updating."

As Melody and LT ate, Bellamy continued with his report. "I have taken the liberty of making inquiries about the installation of an updated system, and it should be available by Monday morning. If it is acceptable to you and agreeable to Miss Melody, Mrs. Bellamy, and the girls will return to your house, Mr. Chadwick, and I shall remain here until the morning when I will return to oversee the barbecue."

LT nodded his agreement. "I sent you a text message with some info in it. Please look into it for me. I think you staying here would be ideal. If you need anything, just call. After the dinner is cleared, the ladies can return to my house. Tomorrow will be very busy, and I'm sure they want to get some rest."

Bellamy agreed and left the room.

Melody looked at LT and asked about the staff again. "I know you said Bellamy was Special Forces or operations, but what about his wife and the maids. They're sisters, the maids are, right?"

LT put his fork down. "Mrs. Bellamy was a cook before they were married. She worked in a restaurant near where Bellamy was stationed, and he used to drop in two or three times a week to eat her food. He was at his final duty station before retirement. He asked her to marry him and she accepted. When he went to butler school in London, she did a course in European cuisine."

Melody interrupted. "It just seems so strange to call him Bellamy and her Mrs. Bellamy."

"Oh, well, that is an old form of address going back quite some time." LT said. "The cook was always referred to as "Mrs." even if she had never been married, the same as a housekeeper. If it feels clumsy to you, just call her "cook." It's up to you to do as you wish."

"For the girls, they are sisters," LT continued. "They have been in the United States for a long time. Their mother and grandmother had been "in service" as they say, for years before they married. A British couple had brought them to their home in New York, along with a house manager. The house manager turned out to be less than honest, and the three were let go. The girls wanted to stay and got a job with one of the Harris families here in Houston. A few years ago, the girl's employers sold up and moved to San Diego. That's when I hired them. As I told you, they do a great job, and you'll never even notice they're around."

"Hmm, I still don't know if all of this is even necessary, but I'll give it a try." Melody was just finishing her wine.

"There are a few other things you should do." LT offered to pour more, but Melody put her hand over her glass. "When we were doing the walk through, I noticed your bedroom. Now when your mother was alive, she never moved out of the room she had shared with your father. The two master bedrooms are just sitting there empty. Those rooms should be cleared of your great-grandparents' and grandparents' things. I want you to pick one and move into it. You need to start living in this house like you own it, not just as a passerby." LT pushed his chair back and held Melody's for her.

Bellamy came into the room. LT looked at him and caught the nod he gave his boss. *Good man*, he thought. He's started the ball rolling on the inquiry into, Lord Arthur and Lord Alfred. Perhaps before he talked to Melody further about her reasons for leaving England early, he would see what the investigators had to say about the two men.

"Bellamy, we'll have some coffee and brandy in the study and then you can take the women back to my house. I'll stay here until you return." LT turned to Melody. "You go on in, and I'll be right with you."

LT held out a set of keys for Bellamy. "Take these and you'll need to have copies made. You also need to get the code to the gate changed as soon as possible. I have no problem that Tommy Hernandez and Manny Marquez, the garden service, has the code, but it is no telling who else may have it. Also, see what you can do about getting a detailed list of what you need from New York before we leave. It would be nice to have an idea of the extent of the missing items before we restock. Other than this, let me know if you think of anything."

Melody was sitting across from the old map of Houston when LT came back into the study. "Impressive, isn't it?"

"Tell me, I'm sure those parcels of land have something on them, does the estate own that many building and houses?" Melody asked.

LT sat in the wingback chair next to Melody. "In most cases, the estate only owns the land, but it's on a long lease." LT saw the strange look he got from Melody.

"Alright, let me explain it this way," he said. "You see this parcel? This is under a post office. When the government wanted to build it, your great-grandfather told the government they could lease the land for ninety-nine years, and when the lease was up, they would pay fifty percent of the current rate to sign another lease for twenty-five years. At the time, the procurement office thought this was a good idea so they signed. Now, for the ninety-nine years, the government, at a set rate plus a percentage of increase every five years, has occupied the land. So, say for example, they originally leased the land for $100. Every five years, the lease money would increase by 3 percent. Now, think what the land was worth when the lease was up a few years ago."

Hmm, yes, Melody could see that and made the calculations. "Wow! Are all of these parcels like the post office?"

LT laughed. "No, girl. These three, in the future medical center are currently parking garages the estate owns. They are very profitable. However, when the hospitals they are attached to want to expand, and they will do that, they can only go up on their current buildings or buy the garages and expand there."

LT pointed to another area on the map. "Here in the area around Rice University well, this was something started by your great-grandpa. He had what would have made two city blocks. But instead of pushing the street on through, he built sixteen row houses, eight to a block, four facing north and four south. They were similar to Boston Brownstones, like the ones he remembered from his time at Harvard. An alley down the back gave each house access to a double garage with a one-bedroom apartment above it, and the Brownstone in front was a three-story, four-bedroom house. They had been leased to university professors. Your father decided to get out of that particular landlord position and in 1980, refurbished them and sold them as condos, but the land underneath the condos belongs to the estate."

"I'm not quite sure if these parcels are all part of the estate anymore." LT pointed at some red patches just down the road from Farr House in River Oaks, "but these are separate family homes. They are special cases. The houses, the ones the estate still owns, belong to elderly friends. In fact, I think they are all widows. They're people the family has promised to look after. As each house becomes vacant, the house is refurbished and sold or else, if there are ready buyers, simply sold. It's something the Farr family has done without much input from outside."

Melody looked at LT. "Special, how?"

"Look, as far as I know, they are people who the family has promised someone they would look after. I know one of the women is the widow of a friend of your granddad's who also didn't make it back from the war. They had no children and when his parents died, she stayed on in the house. Your great-granddad had promised her father-in-law she could stay in the house. The man sold the property to the Farr family for a good price with the stipulation she could remain there. I can tell you, the value of just the land under that house is much more than it has cost to let her live there all these years. When she passes on or has to go into a full-time nursing facility, the house will come to the estate and be sold."

Melody thought for a long time. "And you say there is more information about the estate than just this?" Melody waved her hand at the map. "Is this most of it, half, or what?"

LT looked a little sheepish. "Let's just say there is more than this and leave it there for this evening. I hear Bellamy coming, and you need your rest. Barbecue tomorrow! I want to see you as soon as church is over!"

Melody got up to see LT to the door and said, "I have to come home and change before I come to your place. There is no way I'm wearing my good Sunday things to your party." She laughed. "I am kind of tired. So, you, sir, can leave and get your beauty sleep too!"

Sunday was bright, clear, and unseasonably warm for this time of November. This was going to be the perfect day for LT's last barbecue. Bellamy left early to help with the preparations but checked in first to make sure Melody did not need anything before he left.

Melody always looked forward to church. Like her mother before her, she did not eat before taking communion, and this Sunday was no different. Melody talked to Gina before she left to come to church, and the girls decided they would meet after the service to change from their Sunday church clothes to picnic togs at Farr House.

Before Melody could leave, however, she saw Jose' walking through the kitchen with a couple of men in work clothes and carrying plumber's bags. "Miss Melody, my cousins are here to fix the fixtures in the apartment over the garage so the girls can move in. Also, LT said you would be moving into one of the master bedrooms on the second floor. Can you please show me which one?"

Melody nodded and turned back toward the stairs. She had thought about which of the rooms she would like to have and thought the one her grandmother had used would be best. It had originally been Richard and Lucy's suite when the house was rebuilt after the hurricane. They had both died in the rooms, and her grandmother had lived there for the years she had been resident in the house.

It wasn't that the room was locked or anything, but she just never went in it. The first time she had been in the room for years was during the walk through with Jose' and LT the previous day. Large double doors opened silently to a darkened room. The light switch was somewhere on the wall, but she could see just enough through the lined draperies to find her way across the open space from the door to the windows.

Melody pulled the drapes back and sunshine flooded in. "I'll be taking this room."

Jose' looked around, opened a drawer to the Art Deco waterfall-designed furniture and saw the thing was full. "All of this stuff should be removed, the carpet will need to be rolled up and the furniture taken out. We'll redo the hardwood floors. I need to check the moldings, and the electrician will make sure everything is safe. Can you get this stuff empty in a day or two?"

Melody nodded. It was a good thing the maids would be coming They could help her box all of it, and put them in the attic. She turned back to Jose'. "I'm almost late for church, but it will get done. I'll see you at the barbecue."

Jose' laughed. "I wouldn't miss it, especially when LT's cooking. See you there!"

Melody had barely slid into the pew next to Gina when the processional began. Everyone stood and sang to the accompaniment of the big organ. It wasn't a pipe-organ like some churches had, but it filled the church with music. And that was its main purpose. Melody and Gina both liked to sing, but neither was very good, and they knew it.

As the Rev. Eric Grey began the Holy Communion service, Melody slipped to her knees with the rest of the congregation. She had been in this same pew almost every Sunday for as long as she could remember. From Richard and Lucy Farr up to and including her parents, this had been where the Farrs sat. And, before her mother passed away, Melody had shared the pew with her friend, Gina.

Melody had known Gina since the day they both started college. Gina was originally from Colorado, but her family moved to and lived in Oregon when she left for school. Within a month of her leaving, Gina's mom and dad filed for divorce. To be so far away and the divorce coming so soon after she left, it almost devastated her. Melody helped Gina get through it.

Melody's mother had made it a point to invite Gina to every holiday, celebration, and birthday. Finally, after almost three years, Gina wanted to see her parents and flew to Oregon. Gina had never talked about what happened that weekend, but it was the last time Gina went to Oregon. Melody and Gina celebrated their graduation together, but neither of Gina's parents came.

Two years after graduation, Gina finally told Melody that part of what had helped her through the trauma with her parents was going to church with Melody and her mother every Sunday. Gina's family had never been regular churchgoers, and when they did go, she felt no one knew just why they were there. Attending with

Melody and her mother, she began to understand what church was all about, and the congregation of St. John's made her feel like part of their church family.

Gina moved to Houston after graduation and took a job with an internet start-up company. She became their head buyer for fabrics and a world traveler. When the two friends were in Houston, they usually were in church together on Sunday, so today was just like normal.

After the service, Gina and Melody headed back to Farr House to change for the barbecue at LT's. Gina used one of the first-floor bathrooms, and Melody headed to her room. She saw the door open to her grandmother's suite and decided to peek in after she changed.

The bed was gone, and the large, circular Aubusson carpet it had always sat on was rolled up and waiting to go to the cleaners. Jose' heard Melody come in and joined her.

Jose' pointed to the open door on one wall. "This bedroom has two bathrooms and two very large walk-in closets. Do you want to keep it that way or go for the extra space and take one bathroom out and make it into more closet space?"

Melody chuckled. "I think I want to keep the two bathrooms. Those large closets are actually dressing rooms, and it was designed as a his-and-hers. Grandmother never used it like that, but my great-great-grandparents did. There is also a sitting room through here." Melody walked to two of the curved panels in the wall and pushed them. A bright little sitting room with its own fireplace was revealed. One wall had windows that looked out on what had once been extensive gardens.

Jose' gave a low whistle. "I have never seen anything like this house before. Like the ones in the study, the doors to this room fit so well together they are barely noticeable. But you need to let me know what you want in these two baths."

Melody turned her attention back to the bathrooms. The door that led to the bathrooms and dressing rooms was also a "hidden" door, like the one to the sitting room, but it was open. It revealed a short hall with two doors leading off from it. The one on the right was mirrored on the left and revealed a bathroom, which also led to a dressing room. Except for the age of the bathroom fixtures and the fittings in the dressing rooms, the sizes of the rooms were the same.

"I think I want the room on the right. It will need to have all of Grandmother's things removed, but it looks like this was the ladies' dressing room anyway. The other has tie racks, trouser hangers, and whatnot. So, no, let's do this one. As for the bathroom, it does need some updating. Oh, and when you put the new cabinets and sinks in, make sure you put them at the right height. I'm taller than Grandmother and need them about the same height as the ones in the kitchen."

Jose' was taking notes and nodding his head. "LT mentioned the idea about the cabinet height. I'll get that on the list. Everything will be taken care of."

Melody smiled, "I know you will, and now, are you going to the barbecue or not?"

Jose' closed his notepad and slipped into his back pocket. "I am leaving now. I was in Mass at 6:00 a.m., so I would be ready to eat LT's barbecue. My wife is meeting me at LT's with the girls. We'll see you there."

Melody and Gina were each going to take their own car to LTs, and Gina had left after changing her clothes. Melody had one more stop to make before she joined her.

St. John's had a sizeable cemetery on the side of the church opposite the road. It was a quiet place with a couple of live oak trees to shade the graves and the people who came to visit their loved ones. The Farr family plot had a low wrought iron fence around it and in the center, a Celtic cross stood about five feet tall with the name Farr chiseled into the base.

Melody's great-great-grandfather, Richard, had commissioned it when Miss Lucy died. The headstones for Richard and Lucy were almost identical and marked her death two years before his. On his right were his son, Avery, and his wife, Constance. The left side was empty. It was supposed to have been for Annis Farr. She'd married Chester Lowell, and when they died, old man Joseph Lowell insisted his son and wife be buried in a plot on the Lowell home place.

Next to Avery and his wife, was the plot where they buried an empty pine box to represent the body of their son, Charles Arthur Farr. He had died on D-Day +2, and his body was never fully recovered. What there was of him was laid to rest with hundreds of other GIs in cemeteries in and around Normandy. Next to the empty box with its headstone was Melody's grandmother, Mary Catherine Farr. A new row was added when her father passed away, and her mother had a bench put in so she could sit and visit her husband. Charles Andrew Farr, Melody's father, had a newish headstone that was shared with his wife, Melody's mother, Evangeline Louise Fitzhugh Farr.

Every Sunday, Melody would come and visit the family. The grounds were well cared for, but there was always the stray leaf or weed that tried to invade the perfection of the occupant's eternal sleep. Usually, she would simply sit on the bench and say a prayer.

Today, however, a noise and some movement behind her interrupted her thoughts. Melody turned and saw someone walking in the quiet of the churchyard. Tall, slender, with blue jeans, leather jacket, Stetson, and boots; she guessed he was visiting family. The man turned when he heard Melody move.

Seeing a young lady, the man took off his hat out of respect.

Melody saw dark blue, sapphire-colored eyes, short-trimmed blond hair, and a ruggedly handsome face. She was never good at guessing ages, but she figured he must be about thirty-ish.

"Hello, uh, Miss? I'm trying to find a family plot here and, well, could you help me?" His voice was almost unaccented, but if Melody had to guess, he wasn't from "back East."

"I would be happy to help. What family are you looking for? We have several..." Melody's voice trailed off. He must think she was strange with that last remark, but he wasn't that sure of what he was saying either. "Uhm... I'm Melody Farr, and this is my family. Which is yours?"

The man noticed a slight blush as she talked and was surprised. It had been a long time since he had seen a girl blush. The closer he looked, the clearer it was that this girl was really very beautiful. It wasn't the kind of in-your-face beauty from the magazines but more of a lasting kind of beauty. Melody stood, and he noticed she was tall and willowy but curvy also. In the blue jeans, leather jacket, and hat that she wore, she was quite a good looking girl.

"I'm looking for the Higgins family. I understand there is a Jeremy Higgins and his wife Abigail buried here." He took his eyes off Melody's figure and looked her in the eyes. "He and my great-great-granddaddy were brothers. I don't usually get to Houston with any time to spare, but I have time today, so I thought I'd use it looking for them."

Melody pointed to the two head stones near the rear of the church. Jeremy Higgins and his wife were buried in the churchyard, but none of their children were laid to rest with them. The later generations had their own section where they put their loved ones when they passed. "You'll find them right there. If you have any questions about them, just ask me. Uh, mister, uh, you didn't give me your name."

"Oh, I am sorry. I thought I had. My name is Jeremy Luke Higgins and I was named after my great-great-granduncle." Jeremy bowed his head to Melody and fidgeted with his hat. "Thank you for your help."

"OK, then, you're welcome. I, uh, well, where are you from, if I may ask?" Melody was getting a little flustered under Jeremy Higgins's constant gaze.

"Right now, I'm in between places. I was born in Oklahoma, but for the last few years, I've been living a lot of places. Why?"

"Oh, uh, no reason. Well, it's just that there is this barbecue today and there will be a lot of Jeremy Higgins's descendants attending. I was just wondering if you'd like to go. It's over at LT Chadwick's place, and, well, it's pretty much open invitation. I could tell you how to get there."

Jeremy smiled. "Is that *the* LT Chadwick of Chadwick Holdings?" Melody nodded. "Well, I guess I'd like that. Let me check in with my deceased relatives, and you can tell me how to get there."

Within five minutes, he had taken a couple of pictures with his phone of the headstones he was interested in, and Melody had given him the address. Jeremy was riding a motorcycle and he followed her in her car.

LT's place was only about three miles down the road, and when they came up to the gate, there was a car ahead of them. Melody's car and Jeremy's motorcycle passed through without being announced.

Bellamy knew everyone who ever came to LT's parties and he had never seen the man on the motorcycle. Melody, however, went on through and waited for Jeremy to introduce himself at the front door. Once inside, the two walked through to the veranda, pool enclosure, and outdoor kitchen combination. The outdoor area contained within the lanai was huge.

Bellamy tapped the information on Jeremy into a computer and waited for the results. If the facts he had seen were adverse, he would have quietly had the man leave, but the data that came up was very good from a security standpoint. He would be sure to inform his boss about it.

Melody saw Gina and gave her a wave. Her friend was talking to a tall, rusty-haired man Melody thought might be part of the Harris family. She would find out later if her guess was correct.

LT was holding court by the barbecue pit, and Bellamy was whispering something in his ear. LT watched as Melody and the young man she had met at the cemetery approached and hoped his face didn't give away anything but a big smile. Turning to Bellamy, LT asked that he fetch a drink for Melody and find out what the man with her would like to drink.

"Melody, the meat is just about ready to eat. This brisket has been slow smoking since early this morning and Mrs. Bellamy has made us some really fine side dishes. Bellamy is getting you a drink. Why don't you see Gina for a few moments, and let me get acquainted with your new friend?" LT pointed to where Gina was and Melody headed in that direction.

As soon as Melody was out of earshot, LT turned his attention to Jeremy. "So, Bellamy tells me you're a Marine. Just passing through or are you planning on staying for a while?"

Jeremy turned his dark-blue eyes to LT. "I suppose you could say I'm just passing through. My work with the Marines brings me to Houston quite often for consultations. This is just the first time I've had some off time to visit the churchyard and look for my relatives."

Bellamy brought Jeremy a beer and after taking a good-sized pull on the bottle continued, "Most of the time I am outside the country, so when I'm "in-country" it's nice to catchup on life outside of a war zone."

LT stuck his hand out and shook Jeremy's hand. "I'd like to tell you to visit here whenever you're in town, but this is the last day for me in this house. It goes on the market tomorrow." LT chuckled, "I do have an apartment not far from here, but it's just my bachelor-pad."

LT's face turned serious again. "If you don't mind, what do you do for the Marines or is that classified?"

Jeremy fiddled with his beer a bit. "Well, some of what I do is classified. Mostly, I have a team of experts who are Marines that give advice about oil fields, refineries, and petroleum production. Most of the people in the Pentagon, as well as troops on the ground, don't know that much about such things. Oh, they know about putting gas in a vehicle, changing the oil, or maybe even what an oil storage tank looks like. However, when they get into production fields or refineries, they don't know what to do or look for. That's where we come in. And, I am also in and out of Houston, Dallas, and Tulsa doing consultations with the energy companies here in the States."

LT smiled. He had heard of such teams. In fact, a young man who worked for Chadwick Holdings had come from just such a group. The work they did was little known but vital to the military's work in the war zones of the Middle East. "Sounds like fascinating work. You just go ahead and mix and mingle. Melody will introduce you to the crowd. I hope you enjoy the barbecue."

LT turned back to his pit as Jeremy left to join Melody. Bellamy returned with a fresh drink for his boss and LT instructed Bellamy to look into the young man further. "Find out all you can about him."

Melody and Jeremy moved from group to group as she introduced him to the attendees. Many of the people enjoying LT's barbecue that afternoon were distant relatives, and it was interesting for Melody to watch the interactions. Slowly, piece by piece, as Jeremy talked to the various people, he related some of his own family's history.

Jeremy's namesake, the brother to his great-great-grandfather, George Adam Higgins, had originally come to Texas with his brother. They carved out a ranch from the post-Civil War state just after it had rejoined the United States. Both men worked hard and sacrificed much. His great-great-granddaddy married and had a couple of children. A bad winter with little protection from the bitter cold was too much for them, and pneumonia took his family.

That's when George and Jeremy had their falling out. No one has ever been able to determine exactly what had caused the rift between the two brothers. An aunt of Jeremy's had worked on a family genealogy, and her study of letters and journals revealed nothing. Jeremy and the rest of his clan figured it was the result of losing his loved ones and his brother was the closest person with whom he could argue.

George had gone to California, but after a few years found it wasn't the right place for him. He then headed for the Dakota's, but the bone-chilling cold reminded him of what had taken his family. Finally, he bought a homestead from a man who had settled it in the Oklahoma Land-Rush. It had a house cut into a berm with a sod front, a spring-fed pond, and the land looked good. A grove of pecan trees stood near the house, and the ground was littered with the nuts that had dropped.

On one side of the land, another man wanted to sell his parcel also, so George doubled the size of his holdings. The extra acreage he bought wasn't quite as nice as the first one, but it would do for grazing. His sons and grandsons would find the real boon in the oil and gas wells that would sprout on the land.

Jeremy's great-great-grandfather had missed his brother, and when he married again, he named one of his sons for the brother. The name "Jeremy" has since been given to a son in each succeeding generation. Now it was the turn of Jeremy Luke Higgins to bear the name of the long-lost brother. When he would get back to his hotel, Jeremy wanted to e-mail his cousin, George, the news that he had found the other branch of the Higgins family. Melody noticed that while Jeremy would talk about people in his family that were long dead, he wasn't saying anything about himself or any living relatives.

More than two hours into the barbecue, the food had been eaten, copious amounts of beverages drunk, and the dessert bar had been reduced to crumbs. Melody was ready to leave but didn't want to go without saying good-bye to LT. And, while Jeremy had exchanged contact information with almost everyone at the party, he hadn't even asked for her phone number. Jeremy was at her side, but once she got in her car and went home, she would be leaving him behind.

Melody and Jeremy walked toward LT. "Pinky," as soon as she said it, she could see the playful grimace on LT's face. "Sorry, LT, I have a lot of things to do tomorrow so it's time for me to get back home. It was a lovely party, and I think a wonderful send-off to the end of your residence here. I only hope the next family can appreciate what a fantastic barbecue setup you have."

Jeremy looked at LT. "Pinky? Is that an inside joke?"

LT laughed, "Young man, before this full head of hair turned white, it was a light red, the mark that all Chadwicks and Harrises bear. When I was in school with her father, Melody's dad used to tease me by calling me 'Pinky,' a name one of my brothers had given me when I was still a baby. Unfortunately, the moniker stuck, and Melody is one of the few people who still call me that."

LT turned back to Melody. "The girls have just about finished with the cleanup. They should be at the house in the next couple of hours. They have keys and the code to the gate, so you don't have to worry about letting them in. Jose' told me he finished fixing their rooms and said you had chosen a master suite. I guess that is where you will be working tomorrow?"

Melody nodded. "I will. Those were Grandmother's old rooms and before that, my great-great-grandparents' rooms. It looks like no one has ever taken anything out of there in all these years. I'll be glad to have the girls to help. Do you have any more information about the trip this next weekend?"

LT grinned. "Nope, but my secretary will contact you sometime tomorrow with the details. Are you taking Louisa with you? Anyone else?"

Jeremy had started fidgeting and Melody wanted to end the conversation. "No, just Louisa. Anyway, it's been fun and the barbecue was fantastic." Melody got on tiptoes to plant a peck on LT's cheek.

LT gave her a hug in return. He put his hand out for Jeremy to shake. "Young man, I'd appreciate it if you could stay for a few minutes. I didn't get much chance to visit with you earlier." Turning to Melody, "You go ahead. Drive safely."

As Melody walked away, LT was busy talking to Jeremy.

LT motioned for Jeremy to sit in one of the poolside chairs. "So, what do you think of your distant cousins? Oh, and there are a lot more than were here. There are the Chadwicks, Higginses, Lopezes, and Harrises out on the various ranches and other cities. There are also several, especially from the Higgins family, at the hospital or doctoring somewhere. At last count, there were three from the family who were military doctors, five or six are in the services, and a couple who turned lawyers and went to Washington. We had a cousin that ran for congress, but he only served one term. He's back on the ranch and happy to be out of politics."

Jeremy shook his head. "We never really looked at this part of the family. I guess my aunt Celia never thought to go beyond the immediate family when she was working on the family genealogy. It was a hobby with her, so I can understand. I have a cousin, George, whom I want to tell about all the people I've met." The young man looked around. "He won't believe all the family, although distant, we have here."

LT offered Jeremy a refill on the beer. "No, I really need to get going. I'm staying at the hotel over near the George R. Brown Convention Center, and I don't need to be picked up for drunk driving. It would look bad on my record."

LT's eyes lit up, "Why don't I have someone take you back to your hotel, or if you like, you can stay here. I have plenty of room, well, at least for tonight. Anyway, that is one thing I wanted to talk to you about. How long are you staying and if you're leaving, when are you coming back? I do have my bachelor pad, but it has five bedrooms. So anytime you want a place to stay when you're in Houston, my door is always open."

Jeremy smiled. "That's a fine offer, sir, but I never know when I'll be here or for how long. I know this current trip is ending day after tomorrow."

LT took charge. "It's settled, you're staying with me. I'll have someone give the hotel a call, get you checked out, and your things moved over here. It will give us a chance to get to know each other. Tomorrow when I move to the apartment, then you can just go there too."

LT wanted a chance to find out more about this young man. If he was as impressive in person as he was in the report from Bellamy, he might be someone to keep an eye on for future employment. Melody seemed to warm to him and that in itself was a reason to keep Jeremy close.

Melody turned into the driveway of Farr House and waited for the electric gate to close behind her. The party had been fun, but she had a mound of work to do before LT took her to New

York. She also wanted to look around for more of the information about her family that she wanted for the work she would be doing in England.

Hmm, England, that was a long way away, in both space and time. She hadn't thought about her cousin Arthur or Alfred the whole afternoon, and now she felt almost guilty for having let them slip from her mind. She wanted to remember to check if Alfred had sent any IMs while she was gone or if maybe there was a voice message on the home phone from Arthur.

Melody slipped her key in the door lock and realized this would probably be the last time she would come into a deserted, darkened house by herself. The heels of her boots sounded hollow on the floor as she made her way across the room to the security keypad. Light from the fading day and the porch lights streamed into the foyer from the large, leaded glass windows located over the front door, and they deposited just enough light for her to see.

After punching in the code that reset the house alarm, she sat on one of the polished chairs in the foyer to take off her boots. She then padded across the floor in her stockinged feet with her cowboy boots in her hand toward the stairway and headed up. Melody had just reached the top of the stairs when she heard the familiar *ping* of her computer indicating she had received an IM message.

It was Alfred. She put the boots in the closet and signed in to talk to him. No sooner had she done so, she felt her cellphone vibrate in her pocket. Arthur was on the phone.

While typing a greeting to Alfred with one hand, she answered the phone. Putting it on speaker she laid it down while she talked to one man and typed IM messages to another. "Hello, it's getting a bit late for you. How are you?"

"I'm doing well. I got a call today from the trustee of your estate, and he tells me you will be staying in Houston until, oh, maybe March or so. Right?"

Melody stopped her conversation with Alfred to concentrate on Arthur. "Uh, yes, there are several things in the house that need work, and I should be here for them. I hope this is all right with you?"

She could almost hear Arthur frown. "If this is what needs to be done, then it's fine with me. Look, next week, the last Thursday in November is your Thanksgiving, right? Well I was thinking I might come and stay for a few weeks over Christmas. I mean, I can be your guardian in Houston just as well as here in England. What if I came the first week of December and avoided the holiday travel season?"

"Oh, cousin Arthur, that would be wonderful! I would like to show you my home and perhaps you can help with finding the material which is here for the genealogy. You will have to bring your tuxedo. There is a charity ball the first weekend in December, and we are all going. If you're here, you must also go with us. LT is taking me to New York next weekend to get a ball gown to wear and to purchase some things for the house. Oh, do say you'll go to the ball with us?"

Arthur chuckled. "Calm down. Of course, I will attend. It may give me a chance to see some of your local society in action. Can't you wear the dress you had on at Alfred's dinner party in London? It was a smasher if you ask me."

Now it was Melody's turn to laugh. "It seems I need to look like a cross between a Disney princess and a red carpet ready movie starlet for this thing. I don't know why. It's a charity for the hospital so it shouldn't matter, but LT tells me it does."

Arthur had been thinking about Melody in the gray silk since she had left and it would have been wonderful to see her in it again. She seemed to have good taste, and he wondered what the new dress would look like. "All right, whatever you wear will look marvelous, I'm sure. I'll call later in the week with my travel plans.

Take care, my dear, and get plenty of rest. I'll see you very soon. Good night."

Melody said good night to her cousin, hung up the phone, and turned her attention to Alfred. Now that she knew Arthur had been told about her plans to stay in Houston longer, she felt free to share the information with Alfred. His immediate response was one of surprise and sadness. However, when she told him about Arthur's plans to visit, he asked her if he could come too. She told him about the ball and the need for formal attire. He happily agreed the ball would be fun and that he couldn't wait to escort her. She told him he would be a part of the group that was going and she was looking forward to dancing with him. Another half hour of banter between them, and they both signed off. Alfred promised to send her the details of his travel agenda when he had made his arrangements.

It took but a few minutes for Melody to change from her jeans and flannel shirt into a silk robe and heeled mules. The maids had not arrived yet, and she could wear what she wanted. One of the things she had worried about was her "inside" attire. Ever since she had been a child, Melody's mother had wanted her to change from the clothes she wore to school, church, or any outside activity into something more appropriate for the inside of the house. A picture of Elizabeth Taylor in a magazine gave Melody and her mother the idea that a caftan was just the thing. They each had several, and when Melody's mother died, she took a couple of her favorites for her own use.

Melody took a small footstool her mother had kept in her closet and headed for the room that would soon become her bedroom. The doors were open, and the curtains hadn't been closed. The light from the setting sun still gave Melody enough light to find the switch that would illuminate the chandelier that hung in her grandmother's old suite of rooms.

The carpet had been rolled up and put at the edge of the room. The bed, mattresses, and risers had all been removed and had probably been put in the attic with other unused furniture. Her grandmother's writing desk was still in the room, but the chair had already been taken out. Putting the footstool down, Melody headed back to the kitchen to find a trash bag, a cold bottle of water, and something in which to put things left in the room she wanted to keep.

The lights from a vehicle shone briefly in the kitchen window, and Melody walked into the mudroom to see who had come. The SUV from LT's house had arrived with Bellamy and the two maids. Melody opened the door to greet them.

"Thank you for bringing the girls, Bellamy. I was just getting something to put the trash in and some of Grandmother's things in for storage. I suppose we will need some boxes or storage tubs. What time will you and Mrs. Bellamy be here tomorrow? Perhaps you could pick some tubs up on your way over."

"Miss Melody, Mrs. Bellamy and I will be here as soon as we have taken care of Mr. LT and his guest. That should be around nine. The tubs will be sent over by eight and Paul and Glen can get an early start. Is there anything else you will be needing?"

"Oh, there is one thing. Sometime in the first week of December, we can expect visitors from England. Lord Arthur Farr and Lord Alfred Oswin will be visiting. They're probably staying until after the Christmas holiday. I don't know how you handle such things, but please do whatever it is you do to make their stay enjoyable." Melody thought for a second. "And you might want to tell LT about the visitors I know he wants to keep tabs on me."

"Don't worry, Miss. Everything will be taken care of." Bellamy disappeared up the stairs to the garage apartment with some of the boxes the maids had brought. Turning back into the mudroom, Melody picked up a box she had gotten some books in a month or so before her mother died. It would have to suffice until Bellamy could send the tubs over.

Halfway through the kitchen, one of the maids called to her. "Do you want some help with that, Miss, or is there something you need this evening?"

Melody turned to find the girl, well woman, called Pauline or Paul addressing her, "No, I can handle this. You and your sister aren't on the clock until tomorrow. Please enjoy your evening, and I'll see you in the morning. I hope your apartment is all right."

Paul smiled. "It's a very nice place, Miss. Thank you. Glen and I'll be up and ready before the birds! Goodnight Miss."

As soon as he returned from Farr House, Bellamy walked into the study at LT's house. He knew his boss would like to know about the impending visits of the two men from England as soon as possible. He found LT and his young guest, Jeremy Higgins, having a lively conversation over a few bottles of beer.

Quietly, Bellamy waited until his employer turned his attention to him. Once LT looked over to him, he told LT about the plans for their lordships' visit.

LT paused to think. "Thank you for telling me. I suppose it was to be expected. If either man has any interest in her at all, they wouldn't keep away for long. We just need to keep things from heating up too fast."

As soon as Bellamy had left the room, LT turned to Jeremy. "So, young man, why don't you use some of that leave time you've collected and come stay with me? I have plenty of room, you can have a real homey Christmas, get to know some more of your distant cousins, and who knows, you might grow to like us." LT watched as he talked to the man. He was hoping he was making a convincing argument for the newcomer to stay and perhaps take an interest in Melody. "Oh, and do you have a tuxedo? There is a

big charity ball a bunch of our cousins are throwing for the hospital and you need to come. Which reminds me, I have to call my
cousin Fred tomorrow and tell him we need a bigger table!"

Melody stood in the shower the next morning. She did a lot
of thinking in the shower and knew today would be the first day of
a great change in her life. For the first time since before her grandmother died, the house would be full of servants. The only ones
missing were a gardener and stableman. The gardening was done
by a lawn service who also should do the pool work once it was
refurbished, but everything else was covered by either the maids,
cook, or *hmm*, what exactly was Bellamy? A butler, driver, security
guard, he wore so many different hats; she would have to ask him.

As she entered the kitchen, she could smell the coffee and
breakfast cooking. Mrs. Bellamy, in a flowered apron and comfy
shoes, was busy getting the morning meal ready.

"Good morning, Miss! Oh, it's such a fine day, what would
you like to eat and how do you take your coffee?" The table in the
breakfast room had already been laid with a single place setting,
and the serving bar had eggs, bacon, sausages, and toast. "When
you can," Mrs. Bellamy continued, "we need to do the menu for
this week, and it would help me if you could tell me what you do or
don't like. I'm here for you, and it's you who needs to let me know
these things."

Before she could answer, Bellamy came in to announce that
Mr. LT and young Mr. Jeremy had just come through the front
gate and would be having breakfast. Melody smiled and told him
to lay two extra places. Turning to the cook, "Mrs. Bellamy, it's
good you've made enough, it looks like we're having some guests.
Later today, we can do the menus. As for my dislikes: yogurt, tofu,
and raw fish or meat, but I can do most anything else."

Melody took the back stairs to her room, changed into something more appropriate for visitors, and used the main stairs to greet her guests. LT and Jeremy were just coming through the doors when Melody got to the bottom of the stairs. "Good morning, LT, Jeremy, it's a pleasure to welcome you to Farr House, Mr. Higgins, or should I say Captain Higgins?"

Jeremy stepped forward and shook Melody's hand. "Why don't you just call me Jeremy? After all, we've eaten barbecue together. That should count for something!"

LT watched the interplay between the two young people. It looked to him like maybe this young Marine might just be the one. However, time would tell and he still wanted to see her with the English guys. "Melody, you look just great this morning. I've been officially moved out of my house, and Jeremy is going to be my houseguest at the apartment for a while. Seems he's got some leave he should be using, so he'll probably stay right through the Christmas holidays."

Melody had led the way to the sunny breakfast room and everyone took a seat. She had the feeling LT was trying to engineer something between Jeremy and herself, but so far, Jeremy seemed only mildly interested.

Jeremy looked at the plate of food Bellamy had placed before him. "It all looks so good, a lot like my granddad used to do on a Saturday morning. Only thing missing are the hotcakes, but this is all fine." He turned to LT. "I still have to go back tomorrow and request that leave, but it should be no problem. I think I'll be back by next Tuesday or Wednesday at the latest." Turning his attention back to Melody, "I'll bring my dress uniform for the ball if that's all right. It's been to some fancy embassy parties over the years and should be suitable for that charity thing LT was talking about."

Now Melody was sure LT was up to something. Turning to LT, she raised one eyebrow and quipped, "Seems like this will be a well-attended event. Are you sure the table will be big enough to cater to all of your guests?"

LT laughed, "Hey, you can't help me being anxious to show off a pretty girl now, can you? I just wonder what kind of fancy dress you'll find when we go to New York this weekend." For the next few minutes, the conversation turned around the impending trip to restock the house of various items and her dress hunt.

A sharp trill on his cell phone brought LT back to the fact he had a business to care for and he needed to get on with his day. With the breakfast finished, LT and Jeremy left for the Chadwick building and Melody to the room that needed to be emptied for her to use as a bedroom.

In the center of the room stood a stack of storage containers and the two girls, Glen and Paul, who were busy filling them. A smaller pile of document-sized boxes were sitting near the desk and cabinet for Melody to sort through the papers left by her grandmother and before her, her great-great-grandparents. For the next two hours, Melody divided the items between trash, her grandmother's papers, and items left from her great-great-grandparents.

Bellamy came in to announce the arrival of the interior designer. Melody had finished with the sorting and instructed Bellamy to have the things she wanted to keep moved to the study. He was also to show the designer to the suite of rooms she was having redone.

Mitzy Feirst had been in school with Melody for one year during high school. She had left to attend the high school for the arts, received a scholarship to the design institute, and with the help of her parents, opened an interior design studio. For the past eight years, she had worked at becoming the most prestigious new interior designer in Houston.

Mitzy breezed into the room, set her big messenger bag on the floor, pulled out her iPad to take notes, and gave Melody an enthusiastic hug. "Melody, my gracious! I have never been in your house, but you have got to have one of the best double staircases in town. Oh, my, oh my, oh my," looking around the room she was standing in, she gave the Aubusson carpet that was rolled up at the edge of the room a kick and it opened so she could see the color better. "Oh my, this is some room! And the carpet! Please tell me you're going to keep it in here."

Melody was not surprised at Mitzy's enthusiasm; she had been just as bright and sunny in high school. "The carpet will probably stay, unless there is one in another part of the house you would like in here better." Opening doors to show the hall to the bathrooms and dressing rooms plus the concealed doors to the sitting room, Melody pointed out the amount of space the suite of rooms actually had. "The floors are going to be refinished when all of the remaining furniture and things are removed. Other than this, it needs a paint color. You can look around the house including the attics for any furniture, and if needed, we can add some pieces. I just need it ready when I get back from New York next week."

Mitzy stopped in mid-stride. "Next week? New York? Are you serious?" The level of her voice went up with each new question. "It should take at least two to three months to do what needs to be done. But then, if everything is here or can be found locally, and the workmen can do their work on time, well, hmm, maybe, but I can't promise."

By this time, Mitzy was taking pictures, making notes, and formulating a plan. "We need to sit down and talk about colors, fabrics, a bunch of stuff. Show me the rest of the house, and I can see what is here."

Melody began the tour of the second floor, the third floor attics, and finished in the study. They had stopped for a brief time in Melody's current room and Mitzy asked about the various design elements she saw. "How much of this is **you** and how much is somebody else? It will give me an idea of who you are design-wise. It wouldn't do to put a blue person into a pink room. By the way, how many bedrooms are there in the house?"

"There are twelve guest rooms, another master suite like the one I'm moving into, but at the other end of the hall. That makes fourteen, and there are the servants' quarters on the third floor, over the garage, and next to the kitchen. We also have a pool house with two bedrooms, but it hasn't been used in years. It will have to be refurbished before it can be put into service."

In the study, Melody and Mitzy spent over an hour going over design questions and color selections. Melody asked Mitzy if she wanted to stay for lunch, but the designer declined. "Look, I've got to scoot out of here if this is going to be anywhere near ready for you early next week. I'll call later and let you know what progress I've made."

Melody asked Bellamy to show the young woman out, and Mrs. Bellamy came to ask what she would like for her lunch. "Oh, yes, hmm, if you have some of that bacon left I would love a BLT. And, I suppose we should get to the menu items you were asking about."

Mrs. Bellamy sat with Melody and made some notes about her likes and dislikes. There was nothing out of the ordinary, and both were pleased they had the chance to interact. "I am happy to have you and Bellamy here. I never really thought about what it took to run this house or how little of it my mother and I even used. So thank you for being here."

"Miss Melody, I think we will all be quite content here. Now, what about their lordships' visits? Are there any special parties or events planned?"

Melody looked startled. She hadn't thought about that. Would they be expecting her to have something in their honor while they were visiting or would just the charity ball and the Christmas celebrations be enough of a social calendar? "I think Bellamy might want to contact their people to find out what they require, and I'll talk to LT about any parties or events he thinks might be best. I'll let Bellamy know."

The cook left and within a few minutes, Bellamy brought a lovely tray with a BLT, iced tea, and a small salad. Melody smiled. She could get used to this!

Opening the first box of letters she found, Melody got to work on one of the primary reasons she'd returned to Houston from England. The neat, precise handwriting was one she recognized from some correspondence she'd seen in the library at Farr Cottage while she was in England.

Annis's Story

"Father! Oh Father, please?" Annis's pleading voice got louder and more whiney as she tried to cajole her father into giving her what she wanted. "Avery has a motor-car. Why can't I have one also? I'm sure I can drive! Oh, please!"

Miss Lucy, Annis and Avery's mother, tried quieting her daughter. "It's not ladylike to pester your father. Now eat your breakfast. The ladies from the church will be here for luncheon today, and we still have the flowers to arrange."

Annis and her brother Avery were Richard and Miss Lucy's only children. Born in 1885 a mere three minutes apart, Annis was the older of the two. Annis liked to tease her "little" brother, but the brother and sister loved each other and were very close.

Avery, however, was off at college and Annis, who had finished Miss Evangeline Turner's School for Young Ladies, spent her time doing charity and social work with her mother. Annis's father, Richard Farr, the target of her pleadings, was the owner of a substantial Houston bank.

Richard Farr always found it hard to deny his little girl anything; so he relied on his wife, Miss Lucy, to do it for him. Looking down the table at his lovely wife, Richard was still amazed such a bright, talented, wonderful girl should have ever married him. From the day they were introduced by Richard's mentor, Jeremy Higgins, she had and always would be "Miss" Lucy. In Richard's eyes, she would forever be the enchanting seventeen-year-old upon whom he'd first laid eyes.

It was time for Richard to step in. "Sugar-babe, your brother will be back from school in a few days. He can give you a ride in his car." Shaking his head, "I don't know what you two see in those things. Avery can't drive from the house to town without his motor breaking down or getting stuck in a rut."

Hoping to turn things to a lighter tone, Richard thought to ask about an upcoming party his little girl would be attending. "Have you and your mother finished the dress you'll wear for the ball? I hear from Doc Harris his wife, Elbeth, has spent weeks getting his girls ready."

Miss Lucy nodded. "We finished Annis's dress yesterday. Mary just needs to press the overskirt on the day of the ball." Annis's mother smiled down the table at her husband. "Oh, Richard, she looks so lovely in her gown! Our little 'sugar babe'! She looks so grown-up!"

Annis hated the childish nickname, 'sugar babe', her father had given her, but she knew it was out of love for her that he used it so she really didn't mind. "Father, are you sure Avery will be back in time to take me? You did remind him to bring his evening clothes with him, didn't you?"

Richard nodded. "Don't worry so. If he is delayed, your mother and I will take you. We have to be there anyway. Now, I have to get to the bank." Turning to his wife, "I'll be back a little late today. Jeremy is coming to talk about something." Richard kissed his wife and daughter before putting his jacket on. The carriage ride to his office would take at least an hour, and he needed to leave.

Richard had bought the property where Farr House sat before he married Miss Lucy. At the time, it was almost three miles past the last house. However, Houston had grown, and the area he lived next to, which would later be called River Oaks, was still lush and green. The estate, the thirty acres upon which the house sat and the seven he had given for the church, lay just on the outer edge of one of the more sought after areas in the city.

Electricity had come to Houston early on. New York and Houston were the first two cities in the country to build electric generating plants, and the bank building in downtown Houston was fully electric. His private residence would be electrified before summer. A new invention, air-conditioning, was now available, and the bank was fully cooled. An elevator made getting from one floor to the next easy on the bank's customers also. The six-story building that housed Farr Bank was one of the most modern buildings in downtown Houston.

Avery arrived two days before the first party of the "season." Richard had grown up at a time and place where the young ladies of the landed gentry and aristocracy were given a round of parties. Some girls were presented at court, but all had their "coming out" for society to see they were ready and available to be courted. The young gentlemen would go from party to party, dancing, eating, drinking, and eyeing the debutantes for a possible wife. Houston had no court to introduce its young ladies too, but the local society women didn't let that stop them. Instead, they were the "court," and the eligible girls and young men had a whirlwind of parties where they could meet and parents could gauge the crop of suitable partners for their children.

Some families allowed their girls to have their coming-out parties when they were eighteen but not Annis's mother and father. At eighteen, Annis was still studying at Miss Evangeline's school, and until she graduated, would not be given her chance to be presented to society. At twenty, Annis was not the oldest. Miss Sylvia Johnson was twenty-three, but Annis was the age of most of the other girls. Twenty young ladies, three of them from Doc Harris's family, would be presented to society on Saturday evening. Starting with this first ball, the party season would be in full swing.

Many of the girls would have separate parties in the coming weeks. Usually, that was done for two reasons. A few of the families used these events to flaunt their wealth and position in Houston society. There were also parents whose daughters were a little plainer than or not as gifted as the other debutantes, and at their own balls, these daughters would be the center of attention. Annis's parents were not giving her a separate celebration, but she was allowed to attend the other girls' parties if her brother Avery would escort his sister and look after her.

Parents were also a big part of the ball and party tour. If the young lady had an escort, like Annis did, who was an eligible brother or other close male relative, they would go to the ball together and the parents would attend separately. However, while the fathers might join the other men to discuss politics or "men's" subjects and the mothers sat and talked with the other ladies, there was a core group of women whose business it was to watch the young ladies. A girl's honor and reputation was not going to be lost while these ladies kept watch.

Annis had been standing for what seemed like hours on the low step stool while Mary finished the final touches on her gown. The fine white silk, beautiful tatted Austrian lace, and the diaphanous over-skirt that formed the short train looked splendid on her. A corset, unseen but still a fashion must, was tightly laced and gave Annis the perfect hourglass figure. White kid shoes with two-inch heels would make her one of the taller girls at the ball.

But Annis carried her height well, and the curves of her body gave her classic proportions.

Miss Lucy was allowing Annis to wear her new necklace; the one Richard had bought his wife the last time he was in New York. It was a delicate gold filigree with blue sapphires set in diamond clusters. It was an extravagant gift, but the money from the oil wells on the property near Beaumont was flowing and Richard wanted his wife to have the lovely piece of jewelry. On Annis, the sapphires highlighted the deep blue of her eyes and the gold off-set the honey-gold of her hair. Large carved ivory hair-pins held Annis's long hair in place in a smooth French knot. The effect of the dress, jewelry, and hair gave the girl a sophisticated look similar to the sketches in the fashion magazines Annis and her mother had consulted during the dress's fabrication.

A photographer had been hired to take pictures of the family and Annis in particular. Richard and Miss Lucy were going to the same ball but later than Annis and Avery. The group of ladies who had put the party together wanted the young ladies and their escorts early so they could have them practice their entrances as well as where they were to stand before and after their introductions. For the girl who might be apprehensive about being on public display, the organizers could help them through any stage-fright. It just wouldn't do to have a young lady faint or, worse, lose her lunch, because of nerves.

Seated before one of the velvet drapes in the formal living room, Richard was surrounded by his wife and children. The photographer took two pictures of the whole family as well as separate shots of Richard and Miss Lucy alone, Avery in his formal evening clothes, and Annis in her lovely dress. They were a striking family.

Before the young people could leave, Mary brought out a coat, which had been made specifically to protect the special dress during the carriage ride. Once seated, Mary arranged Annis's dress and coat so it wouldn't be mussed during the trip to the ballroom. Avery got in facing his sister, and the coach set off at a trot.

The hotel where the ball was taking place had a grand portico where each of the couples could alight. The ballroom itself was full of flowers, the seating around the edges was plentiful, and a side room boasted a table with punch and dainty finger foods. An ensemble would play from a balcony overlooking the ballroom and two sets of doors that opened one end of the room onto a veranda, which led to the gardens.

Mary Ester Wimpole was the doyen of Houston society, and it was her group of ladies who, each year, sponsored, planned, and executed the ball with near-military precision and determination. Her father had been a British general who, as a young captain, had fought against Napoleon. She had been presented at court during her London season. Her father's posting to India shortly after her coming out made it possible for Mary Ester and her mother to travel to India to be with him. On the ship, however, a wealthy young American gentleman captivated the Honorable Mary Ester Woodford. With her parent's blessing, the young couple married.

Mary Ester and George Wimpole had three daughters. As the oldest neared the age when she should be presented to society, Mary Ester worried her daughter wouldn't have the same advantage as a presentation at court like she had enjoyed. Gathering other mothers who had daughters together, the Houston Society was formed. Young ladies from suitable families were invited to be presented each year. This would be the first year in which one of Mary Ester's granddaughters, Gloria Bradshaw, would be one of the participants.

The girls all lined up next to their escorts. They could hear the ballroom filling with parents and other adults. Each young lady was in white; but some had overskirts, lace, or other items adorning their gowns in a pastel hue. Annis's mother had insisted she stick to the virginal white. The girls wore white gloves, carried a small bouquet of bluebells, and from their left wrist, hung the program/ dance card. As the music played softly in the background, each girl came through the flower-adorned archway with her escort and took her place before the assemblage. Polite applause accompanied each girl's presentation.

The young men who were their escorts as well as any other eligible gentlemen attending the ball carried a pencil or pen on their person. A program and dance card was necessary for making the evening flow. Once the debutants had all been presented to the society in the ballroom, there was a break in the festivities for everyone to be served a glass of punch. While this was being done, there was a rush by the young men to sign the girls' dance cards. Each booklet had the list of dances that would be played. The first was usually a waltz, and a young man would put his name down to be the first to dance a waltz with the girl. The custom was for the first dance to either be between the girl and her escort or the girl and her father.

Annis was swamped with young men anxious to sign her card. Her brother had the first waltz, but as soon as he signed her card, he handed it back and got in line to sign the youngest Harris girl's book. A small glass of punch was presented to Annis while she watched the eager young men signing their names to claim a dance with her. By the time the card was returned, all her dances were requested.

Annis looked around and saw her parents sitting with Uncle Jeremy. He wasn't really her uncle, but he had been a part of her life growing up and she couldn't remember a time when he wasn't a part of their family's life. He was her mother's, Miss Lucy's, uncle by marriage; but his wife, Abbey, had passed away the year before. Now, he was looking so much older since the love of his life was gone.

Judy Harris, the second of the Harris girls presented that day, came to give Annis a hug. "Oh, I am so glad *that* is over! Mother has done nothing but fuss over this for the last year. Gillian, Marsha, and I are just happy to have it behind us. How's your dance card? Mine is full, and your brother still hasn't signed it. I guess he will just miss out!" When Judy paused to take a breath, Annis took the opportunity to tell her how much she liked her gown.

Judy continued to run on until the musicians gave the signal they were about to start the dance. Avery came to claim his sister; and Judy's cousin, Hank, led Judy onto the floor. Every time a dance number finished, the young men would change partners, and the ball would continue.

Mary Ester and her ladies chaperoned the girls but also tried to make sure each of the newly introduced debutants had dance partners. The young gentlemen were not expected to spend their time standing around, waiting for a dance with a girl whose dance card they had signed. If any of the girls was sitting or standing during a dance without a partner, Mary Ester and her minions were there to encourage them not to leave any girl's dance card empty. It didn't always work but few, if any, of the young ladies would leave without having spent some time on the dance floor.

Three times during the evening the musicians took a short twenty-minute break to give the ladies a chance to powder their nose or drink a glass of punch. Tiny sandwiches, delicate cookies, and other items to tamp down hunger were supplied to the participants. During these breaks, parents and chaperones watched their young people, and the open doors to the veranda were carefully guarded.

Almost before Annis could imagine it, the party was over. Many of the young men who danced with her and others who had wanted to but hadn't made it to her dance card early enough to find a spot, came by to wish her a good evening. They asked her, in front of her parents, if they might call upon her. Her mother, Miss Lucy, was the one to agree to their requests. Annis then handed them a card with her address with the day and times when she and her mother were 'at home.' The whole family boarded the carriage for the ride home. Annis was asleep before they left the last of the electric street lights behind.

Avery also found the ball informative. While he knew most of the people who attended, there were a few new faces. One such face belonged to a Miss Constance Juliet Howard. Inside of his jacket pocket, next to his heart, was Miss Constance's calling card.

The lovely subject of Avery's concentration did not live in Houston, but was visiting cousins. He had carefully quizzed his father about any possible relations to the cousins and found there was none. Now, he would have to be very careful about how he would attempt to go forward with the young lady. He had enjoyed two dances with Miss Constance, and during the second and third refreshment breaks, she had accepted his offer of a glass of punch but refused the plate with the sandwiches. When the party was finished, he had asked her uncle Greg Howard if he might call upon her and her aunt. Mr. Howard agreed.

For days before the party, Annis, like all the other girls, had used her finest penmanship to make her calling cards. The stack she had taken in her small purse was gone and the last few young men to come and ask for one had to go away disappointed. However, most of the young men would be at the next party. Before she attended, she would have to make more cards.

The first of the private parties would be at the large Harris home located between Farr House and downtown. Dr. John Harris had married Elbeth Chadwick a couple of years before Richard and Miss Lucy wed. The small rented house the doctor and his wife occupied had to suffice while the doctor built his office and clinic. The large rambling Victorian office building had Dr. Harris's private consulting room, an office, waiting room, surgery, and patient rooms. However, the small house soon became cramped as Elbeth had more children. Plans were made to build an even larger clinic to accommodate Dr. Harris's patients, two new doctors he had hired to help him in his practice, and the four nurses that cared for the patients who stayed in the clinic's rooms.

As soon as the paint was dry on the new clinic, christened St. Luke's Anglican Hospital, Elbeth had workmen meet her at the old clinic to instruct them to make it into a home. Sunny colors, refinished floors, and some room adjustments turned the clinic into a home big enough for the expanding brood. The last two children, both boys, were born after the family made the move to the new home. The couple's oldest son, John Jr., joined his father as a recently graduated doctor when the new hospital opened.

Two of the Harris's oldest daughters had married doctors, and each of the two younger boys was headed to medical school. Richard liked to tease his friend, Doc Harris that he was trying to cover, single-handedly, the need for doctors in the growing city of Houston.

Present day

Melody put the letters and journal she had been working on back in the document box. The knocking at the study door had been insistent, and it had finally broken through her concentration. "Come in!" Melody supposed she would have a chance to get back to her work later.

Bellamy entered, "Miss Melody, I am so sorry to disturb you, but there are men here from the bank to deliver the silver. They need your signature to authorize the transfer."

Melody hadn't known the silver would be coming today, but she was curious about what had been squirreled away at the bank. Bellamy led her into the kitchen and out the service door into the mudroom. A nondescript van was parked in the drive with two men standing next to it. A third man came forward with a clipboard.

"Uh, Miss Melody Farr?" said the man with the paperwork. "I need you to sign for these crates." The man pointed to the clipboard. "If you could please acknowledge each crate as we take it off the truck and then, uh here," he turned to a different page, "when we're done, please sign here."

Melody took the offered documents. Several boxes were listed but it only identified them by box number, not by contents or size. She had no idea what she was getting. "If your men could take them from the truck and bring these into the kitchen, I'll be happy to receive them and sign." Before the man could react, she had turned and gone back into the house.

One by one, wooden crates were brought into the kitchen. Bellamy had gotten a hammer and small crowbar to help in opening the boxes. Melody hadn't seen the back of the truck opened so she didn't know how many boxes there would be. Mrs. Bellamy moved everything from the kitchen island to make room for the men to set down the delivery.

Melody checked the crate numbers against the manifest and initialed the proper blanks for each box. Paul and Glen came in to help unload the boxes as Bellamy opened them one by one. When the last had been put on the kitchen floor, Melody signed the final page and the delivery men left.

Melody was almost speechless. The room these boxes had taken in the bank's vault must have been the reason they were so quick to want them gone. The ringing of the phone helped to break her shock.

Bellamy answered the phone, but the call was for Melody. Taking the proffered phone from her butler, Melody heard LT's voice. "Hi. I was going to call and alert you about the silver delivery, but I was caught in a meeting. Did everything arrive all right?"

Melody shook her head to clear it. "Sure. I'm not surprised the bank wanted the space in their vault back. I had no idea! I thought it might be some flatware, the tea service, maybe a tray or two, but not this!"

LT was laughing. "I told you. Your great-grandmother was a shrewd person. She acquired quite a lot of things from people who bought above their means. Just wait until they deliver the jewelry, then we can talk about what a good little businesswoman she was. Anyway, I'm just about ready to go for dinner. Would you like to come with me?"

Melody looked around the kitchen, caught Mrs. Bellamy's eye, and mouthed the word "dinner?" Mrs. Bellamy grinned. "We have plenty for Mr. LT or if you will be out this evening, I'll just cook for us, whichever you prefer."

Melody turned back to her call from LT. "Mrs. Bellamy has just told me she has plenty to have you here for dinner. I really don't want to go out anywhere. This silver has just arrived, and I'm anxious to see what everything is. Maybe you can tell me about it over dinner. So, dinner here?"

LT was quick to answer, "Mrs. Bellamy is still my favorite cook. I'll be there shortly. Maybe you can get Bellamy to make us a drink before dinner. I can also have a look at that silver. Remember, I haven't seen most of it since before your grandmother died. Even then, it was never all on display. There are probably pieces that haven't been used since your great-grandmother was giving one of her famous dinner parties! See you soon."

Melody handed the phone back to Bellamy, and the opening of the boxes resumed. The sheer number is what surprised Melody the most. There were at least twenty boxes of all shapes and sizes.

The first two boxes held several serving pieces, cloches to cover plates as they were being presented at the table, and chafing pans with their glass inserts and stands. The two large crates on the floor were opened next. They were hindering the movement of people in the work space, and Bellamy wanted to get them out of the way.

When opened, the large crates revealed an assortment of candlesticks, candelabras, and a sterling silver swan that would have been filled with flowers and used as a centerpiece. Although everything had, so far, been cleaned, wrapped in silver-cloth, and carefully packed for storage, all of it would need to be cleaned and polished.

Melody had never understood the strange closet in the old butler's pantry. It was lined with the same kind of silver-cloth in which the pieces they were unpacking were wrapped. Now, however, she knew once Bellamy had spent his time cleaning each piece, it would go into the silver closet. Until polished to Bellamy's satisfaction, however, it would all sit on the table of the pantry.

Three smaller crates had more serving dishes and platters. One had a morning breakfast service for someone eating in bed. The tray had a toast stand, eggcup, small utensils, jam dish with the spoon, and a sterling rosebud vase. A very heavy but smallish crate held four rosewood boxes with flatware services for twelve in each box plus the service spoons, forks, ladles, and more to match. A box with extra tea spoons was also included.

Several more crates had a champagne bucket, ice buckets for the bar or drinks cart, and an odd collection of forks, bottle stoppers, and other items. Finally, the boxes with the tea service were opened. Melody had only remembered the one, the Georgian service, and it was just as she had last seen it. What she had never known about were the other tea and coffee services. A ten-piece service in the Art Deco style of the 1920s came out of one box and in another, a Victorian service with the cake stands, butterfly-patterned plates, and all the other things which would be used for a fine, high tea.

The front gate buzzed, and Bellamy made sure it was LT's driver requesting entrance. With all the expensive items laying out in full view of any and all, Bellamy was being very careful. Since Mr. LT had said he wanted to see the silver, the girls left the last of the items on the kitchen island until LT would have a chance to have a look.

Bellamy left the kitchen to open the front door for Miss Melody's visitor. LT followed through to the kitchen and handed Bellamy his Stetson. Melody laughed when she saw it. "I remember my father telling me the only time you wear your ranch hat at the office is when you wanted to impress "city folk" who still thought all Texans owned cattle and rode horses. Who was it today, New Yorkers?"

LT laughed, "Nope, Chinese businessmen. The holding company has some land they want to buy, and we don't want to sell. They thought maybe a face-to-face meeting might change my mind. It is land which belonged to some of the first members of the family who settled in Texas. They are big tracts, and are not for sale. So boots, hat, and a lit Cuban cigar helped make them understand they needed to talk to somebody else. Our land is still not for sale."

Silently, Bellamy appeared at LT's elbow with a small silver tray holding a bourbon and water. LT smiled at his recent employee and thanked him for the drink. Melody was happy to spend some time showing her guest the silver on the kitchen island and the other items already taken to the butler's pantry. A small box sat on the table in the pantry, and it didn't look as if it had been emptied.

LT picked up the small crowbar Bellamy had used on some of the small crates and pulled off the wooden top. Inside, securely wrapped in silver-cloth, lay a set of sterling silver children's flatware, drinking cup, plate, and bowl. LT looked at Melody. "You're the last of Richard's line. Don't let it end with you, but, make the right decision. And make it count."

Melody covered the contents, put the top back on the box, and smiled at LT. "Don't forget, I'm the one writing their story. Actually, by the time I'm finished, I hope to have written all of their stories. No, I won't, can't forget what my duty is. Not here," pointing to the box of baby items, "nor the end of the line in England."

Melody took LT's arm. As they walked through the kitchen on their way to the study, she asked Mrs. Bellamy how long it would be until dinner. She also asked Bellamy to freshen LT's bourbon and to bring her a scotch to the study.

LT stayed after dinner for coffee and brandy in the lounge. He asked Melody how the work on the house was coming along but Melody, having been occupied with *Annis's Story*, couldn't answer his questions.

"Bellamy," Melody asked, "what progress did Jose' and his men make today on the renovations?"

Without stopping his work serving the coffee and brandy, Bellamy was quick to answer. "Before they left this evening they had removed the old fixtures from the two bathrooms in your new suite. A man came and sanded the floors in the bedroom, another fixed some tiles in the bathrooms, and the carpet was removed from the two dressing rooms. I believe the cabinets in the bathrooms will be removed so they can be made higher. The man Jose' brought to finish the floors will put the first coat of varnish on after the cabinets are removed."

It was LT's turn to question Bellamy. "Is there any reason we can't go up there? I mean there isn't wet paint or something, right?"

Bellamy shook his head. "No reason I know of, sir."

LT and Melody went to look at the room. For Melody, the real size of the space, with all the furniture gone, was striking. The little sitting room with the big windows looked much bigger, and the dressing rooms seemed huge. The two bathrooms without their tubs, washbasins, and parts of the cabinets missing gave the whole suite a devastated appearance. How could it possibly be ready for her to move into early in the next week?

LT's impression of the rooms was very different. For him, the work that had been accomplished in such a short time showed the skill, mastery, and excellence of Jose' and his workmen. The floors in the two bathrooms were one such example.

Each bathroom had tile floors. One-inch, hexagon-shaped tiles in black and white marble had been laid, by hand more than a century previously. Now, the workmen had cleaned the tiles, replaced any that were damaged or missing, and the floors looked like they were new. Cutting the missing or damaged tiles, each one individually, took great skill, but Jose's men had completed the job.

Refinishing the cabinets, installing new fixtures, and replacing the old windows would not be difficult for them to accomplish. Appraising the work already done, LT nodded his head. Yes, Melody would be able to move into her newly updated rooms by the time they returned from New York.

The thought of New York brought the trip to her mind also. As Melody and her guest returned to the lounge, LT took the opportunity to ask her about the trip.

"Oh, LT, I … uh … do I really have to go? Louisa is bringing me a gown to try on tomorrow and if it is all right, I don't need to get anything in New York. I really do not like to shop." The last was said with a little more force than she had intended. Softening some, "Look, I appreciate you're expecting me to go, but is it necessary?"

Melody still amazed LT. He had never known any woman who didn't like to shop. All of his ex-wives were notorious shoppers. A woman who didn't find the prospects of unlimited stores with no spending limit was such an oddity to him. Oh how LT wished other women could be like Melody!

Shaking his head in wonder, LT replied, "I don't get it, but it puts me in awe. No, even if you had a dress, I still want you to be in New York. There are people you should meet there and take Louisa anyway. She might get ideas for other items she'll want to make for you. Besides, your butler and cook are going to get things for *your* house, and you might want to be there. On top of that, your rooms won't be ready until we get back."

Surrendering, Melody put up her hands. "Okay, you have me. I'll go. Just have your people arrange it with Bellamy."

LT laughed. "They already have, my dear. They already have." Setting his empty glass down on the table next to his elbow, LT stood. "I need to get home, and you need your rest. Bellamy will get my hat and see me out. Have a good night and try not to work too hard on your ancestor's stories. I'd look to your own also." He kissed her on the cheek and left.

Melody was up, showered, and dressed by six. The lateness of the season meant the first lighting of the sky was just showing through the windows. She had gotten a cup of coffee from the kitchen and sat in the study at her father's big desk with her laptop.

Alfred was online, and Melody chatted with him for almost forty-five minutes. Nothing really of substance, just a rundown of what he had been doing since their last communication, and Melody gave him an update on what was happening with her.

Bellamy entered and informed Miss Melody that breakfast was in the morning room. A light omelet, small slice of ham, more coffee, and some broiled tomatoes would have to fuel Melody's work until noon. Bellamy put a fresh mug of coffee in the study and left her to continue *Annis's Story*.

1905

The huge Victorian-style home had lights shining from every window, music escaped into the streets around it, and a constant stream of carriages and the odd motorcar deposited guests in their best finery at the front door. Elbeth had erased all traces of "clinic" from the building, and unless a guest knew the story behind it, no one would ever guess the house had not simply been built as a very large home.

With a full staff of servants to see to her guests' wants and needs, Elbeth was able to focus on her daughters. The girls were all very striking for their height, slimness, and the flaming red hair, a family trait. While most of the freckles in the family had landed on the boys, Gillian had gotten more than her older sisters, Alice and Lois, who were already married to accomplished doctors. The other two sisters, Judy and Marsha, who were presented at the ball the week before, had a slight smattering of freckles which didn't detract from their looks.

Each of the girls had received an education through high school but, unlike Annis, had not gone to finishing school. Elbeth invited a remarkable lady who schooled the girls at home to come and live with them. Elbeth herself, brought up the way she was on the ranch, also wanted to learn the fine manners, deportment, and all she saw as the culture of a lady.

Rolinda Juliet Honoria Lewiston, Marchioness of Howell, had been a permanent fixture in the house for the last few years. Her late husband had led a dissipated life of riotous living in London. He gambled and drank away the family fortune, estate, and thankfully, died before he could do much more damage to his family name. His widow, Lady Rolinda, had a small inheritance from her family, which, although not enough to pay her husband's debts, was enough to buy a modest passage to Galveston, Texas.

Lady Rolinda became a professional guest. Some of the newly rich in Houston found it a boon to their social climbing to have a real Marchioness as a houseguest. Elbeth met Lady Rolinda while visiting friends near Richmond. The two women became immediate friends, and Elbeth brought Lady Rolinda home with her.

The friends Elbeth was visiting were rather pleased when she took Lady Rolinda off their hands. Elbeth installed Lady Rolinda in one of the many bedrooms in the house and pronounced to her husband, Dr. John Harris, that their new guest would be staying. Work on the girl's "finishing" began almost immediately.

It wasn't easy, but Elbeth and the girls worked hard at learning what Lady Rolinda had to teach. She was a strict taskmaster and spent hours teaching the girls and Elbeth the art of being a lady. Needlework, flower arranging, the proper way to enter or leave a room, and hundreds of other lessons were repeated over and over again until they were refined to Lady Rolinda's satisfaction. Each of the girls was given music and voice lessons, hours were spent teaching the whole family how to dance, and the change was remarkable.

When the two older girls were presented to society, it was more like a graduation from Lady Rolinda's lessons. Lady Rolinda carefully chose Alice's and Lois's gowns, the right kind of hairstyle was found which would accentuate the best of each girl, and on the night of the party, it was with a tear in her eye that Lady Rolinda sent the girls off to the ball. For all of the difficult lessons, the hours of practice, and the near exhaustion, the girls were ready to meet society at least as fully prepared, if not better prepared, than the other girls who would attended that night.

She had started working with the last three girls at a younger age, and the learning curve wasn't as steep. A week before the ball, Lady Rolinda announced that as soon as the girls had finished the season, she would be leaving the Harris home. Elbeth and the girls were shocked. Even Dr. Harris, when he was informed of the impending loss of Lady Rolinda, was sad to see the widow leave. Everyone had accepted her as part of the family and regretted her decision to depart.

Lady Rolinda, however, as much as she loved the Harris family, had found a new love. She would miss the girls, Elbeth, and life under Dr. Harris's roof, but a widower by the name of Eustace Jones had asked her to marry him. She just couldn't say no. When the Harris family learned of her reason for leaving, they insisted on providing her the wedding.

The night of the Harris party was the highpoint of the season for the girls and Elbeth. For many of the young ladies, the ball gown they had worn at the coming out party was simply recycled with added lace, a different collar, or some change which made the dress seem new or different. In the Harris house, the girls were all very close to the same size, and the girls exchanged dresses with each other. However, because of the importance of their presentation to society, each had a new dress for the ball and another for their own party. They would exchange with each other for other girl's parties, but not for their own.

The festivities were in full swing when the Farr's arrived. As soon as Annis came through the door, a group of young men began clamoring to sign her dance card. Avery slipped away to claim as many dances as was proper with Miss Constance Howard. Richard found the men in the smoking room, and Miss Lucy walked away, arm in arm, with Elbeth.

Dancing got underway almost immediately. Unlike the ball the previous week, at nine thirty the music stopped, and everyone was invited to enjoy a cold supper buffet. A half hour later, the young people were back on the dance floor. A second break occurred at eleven and the ball finished at twelve thirty in the morning. The Harris family's guests were tired when they left.

Avery spent most of his evening with Miss Howard. He sat with her for the cold buffet, bringing her a plate and punch to the settee where they both ate their refreshments. Nothing Miss Howard asked for was too much for Avery. She only needed to glance at the punch bowl and Avery was on his way to refresh her glass.

Annis danced with several young men, but none seemed to catch her fancy. She wasn't exactly bored. Who could be in such a dazzling company of party-goers? But everyone who attended knew this wasn't just a pleasure party to celebrate an engagement or recognize a birthday. No, this was serious business. For each of the single young ladies, it was their chance to find a suitable husband. The bachelors were there to find a wife, and the parents attended to keep an eye on who was pairing up with whom. A suspicious look when a young man's name was mentioned or a smirk as a young lady passed by could kill the chance of finding a successful match.

The train that would take Avery back to Harvard left the station early on Sunday morning. Rarely would the Farr family miss Sunday services, but this would be the final time the son of the family would be leaving for school and each of the Farrs wanted to send him off with love and good wishes.

Miss Lucy had a sick friend from church she wanted to visit. Along with a bouquet of flowers cut from the garden and the cook adding a pie, the carriage took the mistress of the house to spend the afternoon with the shut-in. Richard had just received a new parcel of books from his old friend in New York, Samuel Newhouse, so he stayed in the library to see what gems were included.

Annis put on an old riding skirt, shirtwaist, and fastened her hair into a tight bun at the nape of her neck. The round barn was where she wanted to go, and with her parents occupied elsewhere, now was the perfect time.

The first structure Richard had built on the estate back in the late 1870s was the round barn. Moses Jones, a former slave, had brought a couple of men and a young boy to build it. Long before the architect had drawn the plans for the house or the road cut, and the land given for the church, the barn was designed and built.

Like most structures in the South, the origin of the barn's design was African. As black slaves were brought to the New World, they also brought the knowledge of growing tobacco, showed white farmers in the Carolinas how to grow rice, and built houses similar to the ones they left in Africa. The wide porches, high ventilated ceilings, and low-pitched roofs were cooler in the hot summers of the Deep South.

Moses's crew built the round barn to weather high winds since a low-pitched roof didn't give the winds anything to grab onto. It looked strange, but it had weathered some very strong storms. Additionally, vents built high in the sides could be opened to allow the heat to escape. Moses chose to build the barn on one of the highest points on the estate so that even when Buffalo Bayou flooded all that was stored inside the barn remained high and dry.

Avery kept his motorcar in the barn. Annis had been taking driving lessons from Avery for quite some time. Both of them thought a plea to learn to drive would have been scary for their parents, but if Avery could show that his sister already knew how to drive, it might make it easier for Miss Lucy and Richard to accept.

Learning how to drive included learning to fix the automobile when it broke down. Avery made lessons in repair mandatory if Annis was going to learn from him. Early that morning, the two young people had taken Avery's motor for a drive so Annis could practice one more time before he had to return to Harvard to finish his studies. As they were returning home, Avery felt something off in the motor and told Annis she had to see to it as soon as she could get away to the barn.

Avery was taller than Annis, and the overalls he wore when he fixed the car in his "shop" were large and baggy on her. The old riding skirt and blouse filled out the legs and arms of the white coveralls, and a cap covered most of Annis's hair. All of the tools were right at hand, and Annis opened the two sides of the motor housing. Bending over the machine, she could have easily been mistaken for Avery.

Annis had barely finished the repair Avery had requested when she felt a stinging slap on her backside. The accompanying, "Hey, Avery," was punctuated by Annis's scream. She straightened up and spun around to face her attacker. Her gloved hands were stained with dirt from the motor, and in her right hand, Annis still held the wrench she had been using.

Chester Lowell was dumbfounded. He was prepared to have his friend Avery give him a counter-punch, but a girl? What was a girl doing with a wrench inside Avery's motorcar? His mouth opened, but no words came out.

"How dare you attack me! Who are you and what do you want?" Annis brushed the cap from her head with her left hand and smeared dirt on her forehead. A tendril of hair escaped and curled its way to her shoulder. "Well, speak up, who are you?" The volume of her voice continued to increase.

"Uh … I'm uh … uh … Chester … uh … Chet Lowell. Gee, I'm sorry. I thought you were Avery. I'm … uh … uh …" Words failed him for the moment. The sapphire blue eyes were shooting sparks at him, and the honey gold hair framed the face of a beautiful ivory complexion.

"Well, Mister Lowell, I don't know what you are doing here, but as you can see, I'm not Avery. I'm his sister, Annis. He's on his way back to Harvard and won't be home until he finishes in about three weeks. He will be back for Penny Stuyvesant's party because he is escorting me, and he's promised Miss Constance Howard he would be attending."

At this point, Chet Lowell hadn't done any more damage than mistaking his friend for his friend's sister. Profuse apologies for this mistake, but pointing out that it was, after all, a mistake might have quieted the whole incident. However, Chet and his twin brother, Hector, had lived in an all-male household since their mother died when they were young. His father, Joseph Lowell, had some property near Richmond Road and hadn't really taught his boys that much about women. Perhaps that would account for the next words Chet was finally able to utter.

"Gee, I'm sorry. I … uh … I guess I should have known it wasn't Avery. He's not as broad … uh … big as you are … oh … I mean he's taller … oh … uh …" Chet saw the color rise in Annis's face and then drain. If her eyes were shooting sparks at him before, they were now shooting daggers at him.

"MISTER LOWELL! Did you just call me FAT?!" Annis had forgotten the temporary discomfort of the slap. The idea this Cretan would say she was fat was just too much to bear.

Chet finally saw the wrench in the girl's hand and the look of anger in her eyes. He took a step back, and it broke the mood long enough for Annis to put the wrench down. With a voice white-hot with anger, Annis turned on the man. "You, sir, are a cad! How dare you make such an observation when you don't even know me. I've told you, Avery is not here. Leave! Leave or I'll … I'll … I'll start screaming and someone will come and make you leave!"

As beautiful as the girl was, Chet did know when it was best to retreat. He doffed his cap, and then replaced it while he turned to leave the property. Dealing with Avery's sister was not how he had wanted to spend his Sunday.

Annis watched the man turn the corner and heard the motor of an automobile begin to purr. She picked up the wrench and returned to what she was doing. Her mind, however, remained on the incident. *How dare he*! She was going to have to talk to Avery about the kind of friendships he was fostering. *Fat?!* She wasn't fat. Annis was so furious over his remark, or did he really call her fat? *Hmm, well, even if he didn't say it, that was his meaning.*

Eventually, Annis had to recognize she was finished working on the motor. She put the wrench back in the toolbox, refastened the motor housing, and removed her gloves. She looked down at the overalls she was wearing. Well, she did have to admit the covers didn't allow her figure to show. In fact, the extra fabric of the riding skirt and shirtwaist added padding that would have made her look heavier. Nevertheless, a true gentleman would never have commented on something like that to begin with. For the first time since the incident happened, Annis smiled. Mister Lowell was no gentleman and that was that!

Annis returned to the house shortly before her mother did. Her mother's friend's illness was not something which would be settled in an afternoon, and a distant cousin of the shut-in was coming from Beaumont to help care for her. Miss Lucy was happy the ailing lady would have someone with her all the time. This was the second time she had sat with her, and it was very tiring. Miss Lucy went to her bedroom to rest before dinner.

Richard was still in the library with his new books, Avery was speeding toward Boston, and Annis had nothing much to keep her occupied. It gave her mind a chance to rerun the incident in the round barn. For the first time, her mind focused not on the offense but the offender. Having determined he was not a gentleman, she had assumed he would no longer be worth her time, but her mind was not finished with him yet. Annis picked up an embroidery project she was working on as a gift for her mother, and while it kept her hands busy, it didn't take her mind from her afternoon.

Hmm, come to think of it, he was kind of handsome. He was about the same height as Avery, but although Avery was slender, Chester, or did he say Chet, was more muscular. He was also tanned, a sign he probably worked or at least spent a lot of time outside. He didn't say much. He mostly just stood around with his mouth open, like a cod fish. Annis giggled at that. Yes, a cod fish. His eyes were also nice. They were dark brown, like his hair, but had bright lights within, which gave them depth.

Annis realized her mind was wandering, and when she looked at her handiwork, frowned. The last few stitches were no better than she had done as a ten-year-old. She picked the mistakes out and put the piece back into her sewing basket. She clearly had no head for concentration, so she joined her father in the library. With a good book and her father's familiar presence, Chet or Chester Lowell, faded into the back of her consciousness.

Chet or Chester did recede somewhat. However, Annis would catch herself daydreaming off and on, and the face she put on her daydream looked very similar to her brother's friend's, but her life was too busy to spend much time daydreaming. Avery was due back for Penny Stuyvesant's party, and Annis was working on a new dress for the event.

Because her brother was not in Houston to escort her, she had to miss Lisa Allen and Elizabeth Perry's parties. The Harris girls were eager to recount every dance, describe what each girl was wearing, and list which young gentlemen were attending. After the first half hour of these blow-by-blow descriptions Annis's mind would only half listen, the other half would daydream about those flashing dark brown eyes.

Miss Lucy had found a piece of shimmery silk that had the same deep shade of blue as Annis's eyes. While the debutants all wore white, or mostly white, to the ball where they were presented, some of the girls then began to add color almost immediately for the balls that followed. A few went with pastels, and one or two chose darker colors, but the gown Annis was working on for Penny's party would be much different than the dresses she had worn so far.

The design came from a new fashion magazine which had just been brought from Paris. Most such picture books came via New York or New Orleans and took several months to filter down to the "wilds" of Texas. A client of her father's bank, however, had taken his family on the "Grand Tour" and recently returned. The fashion journal was a gift from his wife to Miss Lucy.

Some of the dresses shown were very daring and would never have been considered suitable for a young lady. There was, however, one sketch that would work perfectly for Annis. The blue silk was picture-perfect for the design. Mary, the Farr's housekeeper, was an expert dressmaker and with the three women working together, the finished dress was stunning.

Miss Penelope Stuyvesant, known to her friends as Penny, was, quite possibly, the most beautiful of the year's debutants. She had a perfect figure, was not as tall as Annis at just under five feet five inches, had sky blue eyes, spun-glass blond hair, and a very light personality. Her parents were not giving her a party because she would have trouble finding a husband from among the available young gentlemen. No, they were giving her a party to show off their wealth.

Penny's older sister, Jenna, had been a debutant three years previously. Mary Ester Wimpole's Houston Society ball had hosted a special guest that year, a duke from Italy. The young man was from a very old but, alas, impoverished family. When Jenna was presented to Duke Paulo Perini-Parma, the two young people were captivated with each other. The Duke's mother, the Dowager Duchess, saw money, and Jenna's mother and father saw a title for their little girl. The couple waited six months to wed, and the union had already produced a baby boy. All of the grandparents were ecstatic.

While no royalty, destitute or not, was attending any of this season's parties, there was a fair-sized crop of eligible gentlemen. Houston did not have the population yet to provide enough to choose from, but friends and relations of local citizens from other parts of the United States did help to fill the deficit. Chet Lowell and his brother, Hector, would have been on any hostesses' list of suitable young men if they had wanted to be present at any of the parties. Until the encounter with Annis, Chet had better things to do with his time; now, she and Penny's party was all he could think about. Hector was finally coaxed into attending with him.

Two days before the party, Avery arrived by train. His days of study at Harvard were complete, and the huge trunks in the baggage car of the train were all he had left of his time at university. A freight-wagon was hired at the station to take the load to Farr House.

Annis and her brother had very few private moments to talk in the round barn the next morning and the subject of Chester Lowell was not part of the conversation. The motorcar and the care Annis had given it were uppermost in Avery's mind. He was very pleased with her work and they discussed when it would be a good time to present her ability to drive and care for a motorcar as a *fait accompli*. Both knew it would probably anger their parents. However the motorcar was the future, and it was better to be ahead of the curve. Together, they decided it would be more prudent to leave the matter until the next week.

Saturday night was the party at Penny's. Avery was anxious to see Miss Constance Howard of Richmond, Virginia. The two young people had kept a constant flow of correspondence going between them and, at least on the Howard family's side, an "understanding" was sure to be forthcoming.

Courtship rituals at the time and in the Farr family were very formal. The first level of interest in a young man or woman was the permission to call. The parents of the young lady would be asked for consent to visit for brief periods and to initiate a correspondence. All visits and letters were sent and received under strict parental or guardian supervision.

If a young couple was ready to advance their relationship, the next step was an understanding. This meant both families were ready to agree the two young people in question were suited to each other, there were no impediments to a possible future together, and the families were in favor of the couple going forward. The period of an understanding may last a few months or it could be years. For most young lovers, the shorter the better was their choice. Only after the understanding would the matter of a formal engagement be addressed.

In the case of Avery and Miss Constance, the understanding period would last for a few years. Richard and Miss Lucy had been watching their son and his pursuit of the young Howard girl. Richard knew her uncle, Greg Howard. They had some business dealings. The prospect of the niece marrying their only son did not worry the Farrs. However, Avery was not ready to be married.

Because Avery was the only son, he was expected to assume control of the bank when Richard was ready to retire or step down. The education at Harvard was nice, but to learn and understand the banking business required more than just studying the Classics or conjugating Latin verbs. Richard had a program of study or apprenticeship laid out, and he expected Avery to pursue this course and not be distracted by a fiancé, wife, or young children arriving. A long understanding would suit Richard just fine.

When Richard began in the banking business, he had taken the money his father had left him and became partners with a gentleman named Samuel Newhouse. Samuel was Jewish and catered to the Jewish community with his bank occupying one second-floor office in an old building that had since been replaced with a new six-story, high-rise office tower. After the partnership between Richard and Samuel was made, the two men had opened a standard bank on the ground floor for walk-in customers, and anyone who wanted to become a customer was accepted.

Samuel had taught Richard a lot about banking in the United States and also about the particular needs of the Jewish community. In 1890, Richard bought out Samuel's part of the partnership, and Samuel returned to New York. The two men had been friends and frequent correspondents for years. Richard arranged, with Samuel's help, a junior position for Avery with one of the large New York banks. Moreover, although Samuel was retired from the banking business, he still had deep contacts in the Jewish banking community in New York. Richard wanted Avery to learn as much as he could about all aspects of both.

Yes, a long understanding with Miss Constance Howard would be necessary, and Richard would not budge from his position. Miss Lucy understood how difficult it was to wait. She had waited for several years while Richard established himself in Houston banking, but she agreed with her husband. For them, the matter was closed. Avery didn't like it, but he understood it was for the best. By the end of summer, Avery would be in New York.

The Stuyvesant estate was gaily lighted. The large grounds were electrified the year before, and every light in the mansion seemed to be in use. Torches lit the gate and the lane which led from the avenue to the Greek-Revival stone house.

Maude and George Place lived just down the road from the Farrs and offered to give Avery and Annis a ride to the party in George's new 1905 Buick. George was dying to show off his new motorcar, and the night of the party, with all of the upper crust of Houston in attendance, seemed to be the perfect place to do so. George also wanted to flaunt it in front Avery.

Before leaving the house, Annis put a long duster over her dress. Miss Lucy was worried that the dirt or maybe even smoke from the car would ruin Annis's pretty new frock, but she needn't have fretted. When Annis and Avery arrived at the ball, the ride had been quick and without incident.

The men helped the ladies out but stayed back to answer some questions posed by other gents who were just arriving. Avery left George to beam over his beautiful car and walked Maude and Annis into the lighted entry hall. The men left their hats, and the women left their coats.

When Annis removed the long duster, it was the first chance anyone other than her mother and Mary had had of seeing her in the beautiful blue silk. The fabric caught the light. The effect was to make the fabric look like liquid blue, a pearl-essence which flowed as Annis moved. Woven in India by a method hundreds of years old, the material was light and supple.

The picture in the Paris fashion magazine had been titled, "Papillion" or butterfly. The short sleeves fluttered like butterfly wings, and the tight bodice was cut into a sweetheart shape. The skirt flowed from a tiny waist and in front, fell straight to the floor. On the sides of the skirt, the light fabric was cut long to make a train and then gathered into an intricate layer of folds down the back. The look, the dress, and Annis were stunning.

Before she saw him she heard a familiar voice call, "Avery!" And Annis knew the man who had inhabited her dreams since the first time she met him, in the round barn, was approaching. Just as he reached Avery's side, Annis turned to find, not the country clod who had struck her when she was working on Avery's car, but a pair of well-dressed, elegant gentlemen who looked identical.

One of the twins stood with his mouth open in a very ungentlemanly like way, but the other simply showed surprise. An elbow to the ribs from one twin to the other closed the mouth, and the one with the surprised look on his face was trying to speak. "I … uh … hmm. Avery … uh … Avery, is this your sister?" The rising redness in his face accompanied his halting speech.

Avery had his mind on finding his Miss Constance, so the introductions were brief. "Oh, yes, well, Chester, Hector, this is my sister Annis. Annis, Chester and Hector Lowell."

Chester stepped forward as Annis offered her hand. "Everyone calls me Chet and Hector here," motioning to his twin, "is just called Hal."

Avery was looking around the room to find his girl, but couldn't. "I never expected to see you two here. I thought this wasn't your kind of thing." Turning to Annis, "These two are a couple of years older than me. We all like motorcars and we have even raced against each other. Oh, but don't tell Father that. He'll never let me drive again, and, if I can't drive, then neither can you!"

A commotion near the front door caused Avery turn and see Miss Constance Howard arrive. "Uh … I … uh … it was nice seeing you, but I need to go sign Miss Howard's dance card before it's all filled." Without waiting for a reply, Avery turned and left.

Chet turned to his brother. "Hal, why don't you go look for the punch bowl? I'm sure you're parched from the long ride in." Hal made a face at his brother and left. Turning his attention back to Annis, Chet locked eyes with her and said, "Hmm, speaking of dance cards, Miss Farr, may I sign yours?"

From her beaded handbag, Annis pulled out her dance card. She was unaware of anyone else in the room, only Chet whose dark eyes held her transfixed as she handed him the card.

Other young men were mingling around and signing the dance cards of the young ladies at the party. Seeing Chet holding Annis's card, they began to ask for a dance. Chet wrote his name on her card and smiled. Then he handed it back to Annis and left.

Looking at the card, she realized Chet had written his name in for each of the dances. Annis couldn't believe her eyes. No one ever took all of a girl's dances, but then, Annis had the feeling that Chet wasn't playing by anyone's rules but his own. The other young men left to grumble about their luck.

Richard and Miss Lucy arrived a few minutes later and found Annis still standing where Avery had left her. Her mother came to check on her, and Annis showed her the card. Miss Lucy had a word with Richard, and instead of spending their time, as they had expected, with the discussion on Avery's future with Miss Constance and her uncle, Greg Howard, the focus became the intentions of Mr. Chester Lowell.

Miss Lucy stayed with Annis while Richard left to find Chester Lowell. He found the twins near the punch bowl talking quietly to each other. Richard cleared his throat to get their attention. "Uh, yes, which one of you is Chester Lowell? I'm Annis Farr's father, and I would like to have a word with you."

Chester set his cup on the table and faced Annis's father. "I'm Chester Lowell and this is my brother, Hector. My friends and family call me Chet and him," gesturing to his twin, "they call him Hal. Can I help you?"

"Uh, yes, Chet, I would like to know why you have taken all of my daughter's dances. I mean, it's just not done. Only engaged couples do that, and as far as I know, you have only just been introduced to my little girl." The penetrating gaze Richard was getting from Chet's dark eyes was a bit unsettling.

"Mr. Farr, I have nothing but the greatest respect and admiration for Annis. That is why I am going to marry her, with your permission of course. Might I call on you tomorrow afternoon to discuss this?"

Richard's face flamed red hot. *Who was this young pup to presume so much?!* "Sir, you are no gentleman if you expect me to hand my daughter over to you like that! You two have only just met and you expect to marry? Nonsense!"

"Ah, well then, at what time tomorrow may I call?" Chet smiled at Richard's back as he left to find his wife and daughter.

Richard was slightly calmer when he reached his family. His face wasn't quite as red, but he was shaking his head. Miss Lucy looked at him. "Did you find him? What did he have to say for himself?"

"Oh yes, I found him." He patted his wife's arm. "He wants to come to the house tomorrow. The silly boy says he's going to marry Annis. I told him he was out of line."

Annis, hearing her name, looked at her father. "But Father, of course I'm going to marry him."

Welcome to Farr House!

The house phone rang for the second time as Melody laid the file aside. Annis and Chet would have to wait until Melody returned from New York. Picking up the phone, Melody answered. "Yes? Oh, right. I'll be there in about twenty minutes. Just give LT a drink and he'll be fine."

One of the maids, Glen probably, had packed her suitcases and set them in the hall. All Melody had to do was change before the trip. LT was in the lounge waiting to take her to the airport so they could leave for New York. Before she left, however, she wanted to check on the progress of the work in the house.

Melody's suite of rooms was almost finished, or at least it looked that way. The rooms she would put Lord Alfred and Lord Arthur in were getting a new coat of paint and generally freshened in the week before they arrived. Mitzy Feirst and Jose`, LT's builder, had been working together so well, and most of the cosmetic work on the house was close to done. The new kitchen cabinets and appliances were going in while Melody was in New York, and the only major item she could think of was the pool.

Dressed in a black suit, Melody was ready for the big city. Louisa had brought her a ball gown from her shop a few days before to wear for the party, and except for some slight changes, it would make a wonderful dress. However, LT insisted she look in New York, and Louisa was going with them to help fit whatever she might find. Bellamy and Mrs. Bellamy would be accompanying them on the plane, but they had gone on ahead with Louisa to the airport.

The business jet belonged to Chadwick Holdings and since some of the trip was for business, it would pass scrutiny with anyone who might question LT using it. Since only family sat on the board, and most of them had used the jet from time to time for trips fishing in the Caribbean or hunting in Colorado, no one would say a word.

The Royal Suite at the Plaza was set up specifically for the kind of staff LT had brought along. The kitchen was perfect for a personal chef, and with Bellamy in attendance, a private butler supplied by the hotel was not necessary. The whole thing would make just the right impression on the people LT was meeting. Louisa had a separate room next to the staff, and Melody was in one of the suite's three bedrooms.

LTs first business meeting was that evening. Having arrived at the hotel just after 7 p.m., there was no time for Mrs. Bellamy to shop and cook a meal, so room service was ordered for everyone. While LT was gone to see to his business, Melody spent the time on the suite's balcony looking out over Central Park and the city beyond.

The night was clear, and the muffled din of the city served as white noise. Melody had her laptop with her, and although the hour was late, she and Lord Alfred Oswin were IM-ing back and forth. Travel arrangements were discussed, and it surprised Melody that Alfred and Lord Arthur Farr, Melody's guardian, would be traveling together. It would make it easier for Melody. However, the two men didn't get on very well together, so to travel on the same plane would make an icy trip.

Melody and Alfred ended their chat and LT came back from his meeting. Bellamy appeared and offered to bring them coffee and brandy. LT and Melody enjoyed their drinks, as the pulse of the city carried on below. Tomorrow would be a busy day, so Melody said goodnight and left to get some sleep.

Breakfast was ready when Melody got up. It was surprising that Mrs. Bellamy could have found everything so quickly and made such a sumptuous meal. In the short time Mrs. Bellamy had worked in Melody's house, Melody had found the lady could do wonders with just about anything. LT was already at the table and starting on the eggs and bacon.

Everyone had a full agenda planned. LT had business meetings all day and the dinner that evening. Melody and Louisa had an appointment at two different stores to look at dresses. Mrs. Bellamy had the formal dinner to shop for and prepare here in New York and Bellamy would be busy getting the items needed for Melody's house in Houston.

LT gave Melody a pat on the shoulder as he left the table and hurried to his first appointment. Melody still had an hour before she and Louisa needed to be at Elan`, the first store LT had recommended for a gown. They would then have lunch before they needed to be at Haverstein's. If there was still enough time after the last appointment, Louisa was desperate to get to a fabric store called Mood.

A limousine took Melody and Louise from the hotel to the first store. The manager greeted them and put Melody in a large fitting room. Several dresses were already hanging on hooks around the room, and Louisa and Melody looked at what the staff at the store had pulled for her. Seeing Melody in person, the manager,

Mrs. Reese, had some additional picks for her to see. The group of dresses was narrowed to three.

The first was beautiful on the hanger, but once on her, Melody and Louisa could see immediately the gown was made for a tall, very slender person with no major bust line or curves. Melody was tall and very slender, but she had a generous bust, tiny waist, and enough curve to her hips that there was no way she could be mistaken for anything but a girl. Mrs. Reese left to pull another dress.

While the manager was gone, Louisa helped Melody into the second dress. It had better potential but was still inferior to the dress Louisa had shown Melody the day before they left Houston for New York. Louisa had one of her girls doing the alterations on the dress in Houston, and it would be ready for Melody to wear to the charity ball if they found nothing in New York.

Mrs. Reese came in with a red dress. Immediately, Melody was drawn to it. Although it wouldn't be suitable for the charity ball, Melody could think of several places where she would like to wear it. Dinner this evening in the suite would be the perfect place. It fit perfectly and needed only the hem adjusted, something Louisa could do at the hotel. Melody paid for the dress, and the store said they would have it sent to the Plaza.

Lunch was eaten from a food truck near the upcoming store. Melody had seen food trucks in Houston, but nothing with as fancy a fare as this one. The meal for her and Louisa cost almost thirty dollars with their drinks, but it was a wonderful Korean barbecue with a Thai chicken salad. She was surprised to find the owners, the husband a Thai, and the wife Korean, highlighting both ethnic cuisines in one place, and it made for a delightful lunch.

The next appointment was in a store that catered more to bridal wear and bridal parties. They did have one very large section for ball gowns, pageant dresses, and unusual gowns that could be used as bridal wear. The dressing room they had set aside for

Melody was twice as large as the one at *Elan's* and was filled with potential dresses for Melody.

The consultant who was assigned to her was past middle-age and had been doing this kind of work since her teens. She looked at Melody in nothing but her underwear, surveyed the dresses already pulled, and started having one of the assistants move unlikely ones from the room. A rose pink was also taken out when Melody had voiced her dislike of pink.

The first dress Melody tried was a dusky blue. It fit well enough, but the color just didn't suit her complexion. The next dress was an emerald dupioni silk that rustled as she moved. It was beautiful, but it still wasn't right. The consultant left to find another dress she thought would work.

Louisa and Melody looked at the other dresses still hanging in the room but in each case the color, cut, or fabric didn't interest them. The consultant returned with a dress bag over her arm. "The owner, Mrs. Haverstein, had to get this one for me. I think this just might be your dress." Directing her commands to an assistant, "Julie, help me hang this."

The assistant lifted the hanger onto one of the hooks, and the consultant removed the bag. Melody caught her breath. The blue, her favorite color, was astounding! The dress itself was a pure ball gown a' la Cinderella, but it was the color!

Melody had, since she was a little girl watching sunsets with her father, been fascinated by two colors of evening. The first was the deep purple which lasts for only a few seconds as the last rays of a red sinking sun mix with the pure, clear blue of a night sky. It only happens at certain times of the year, and Melody remembered it from when she would sit on the patio with her father and watch for night to come. She had been afraid of the dark when she was little, and it was her dad's way of showing her there was nothing of which to be scared.

The second and Melody's most favored color of the evening was the clear, dark blue that remained after the purple. Some people called it midnight blue, but it wasn't as dark as that since there was still white light from the sun. No, it was a blue all of its own and the fabric of the dress had captured it completely.

The consultant helped Melody step into the dress, pulled it up to her waist, and then helped her get her arms into the sleeves. It was a little too big in the waist after the zipper was pulled up, but the length was perfect. The fabric had a slight iridescence that gave the color of the gown a depth of hue Melody and Louisa both loved.

Louisa knew this was the dress for Melody. The one her girl was working on in Houston would be right for another occasion; but for the charity ball, Melody, in this dress, would outshine everyone. Louisa then looked at the waist and told the consultant she would be doing the adjustments in Houston.

The owner, Mrs. Haverstein, came into the room after Melody had dressed. The two women sat and discussed the dress. "Miss Farr, the ladies tell me you looked fabulous in this dress. It is a one of a kind. The designer is or was from Greece, and because of the collapse of the Greek economy, she has closed her business. The dress has been in our vault for almost two years waiting for just the right person."

"Now, let's talk money." Mrs. Haverstein motioned to the dress hanging on the wall. "Since your seamstress will be doing the adjustments, and we have had the gown for two years, I am giving you a discount. Will you be taking it with you?"

Melody pulled her charge card from her handbag and handed it to the lady. "No, I will give you the address of where to ship it. Can you add the overnight FedEx to the bill?"

Mrs. Haverstein gave a big smile. "Absolutely!"

Melody and Louisa left the store, hailed a cab, and found Mood, the place Louisa was anxious to visit. The store had everything a clothing designer, seamstress, or tailor could want. The place was stuffed with fabrics of all kinds, colors, and price ranges. The "findings" department was equally well outfitted. There probably wasn't a button, thread, stay, or lace variety the store didn't have. For Louisa, it was Candyland, Disney World, and the Tiffney of her dreams, rolled into one.

Melody dragged Louisa out of the store before they became late for the formal dinner party. Louisa had to do the adjustments to the red dress Melody had bought before lunch and besides, they couldn't buy everything in the store! Louisa was carrying a small bag with a few items she would need while in New York; the remainder of the items was being sent to her shop in Houston.

The suite was filled with fresh flowers, Bellamy was in his formal attire, and the dining table had been set for six. Judging by the wine glasses, it would be a fairly fancy affair.

Louisa got the dress from Melody's room and marked the changes which she needed to make. "I'll have it back in about a half hour," Louisa said as she left Melody preparing to slip into a hot bathtub. "Are you putting your hair up or down tonight? If you want it up, I bought a great decorative comb at Mood that might go great with this dress."

Melody nodded. "I will put it back, not up. Bring the comb, and we can see." Melody got into the tub, and Louisa left to do the changes. By the time Louisa had finished, Melody was ready to slip on the dress to see how it fit. Louisa tried the comb in Melody's hair, and it worked wonderfully with the dress. The overall look was outstanding. Now, it was time to see about LT's guests.

Louisa went to the kitchen to give Mrs. Bellamy assistance and found she wasn't needed. This would give Louisa a chance for an early night.

Melody could hear the talk coming from the living room of the suite. When she appeared at the door, all conversation stopped, and LT walked across the room to take her arm. All four men were looking at her. "This, gentlemen, is my best friend's daughter, Melody Farr."

The first man LT stopped to greet was the oldest in the room. "Melody, this is Abraham Newhouse. Abe, Melody." While the old gentleman shook her hand, Melody looked quizzically at LT. "Yes, it is the same family." LT looked at Abe to explain. "Melody is a historian and is working on the family genealogy. She has seen mention of your great-great-grandfather as well as the Newhouse & Farr Bank."

Abe held Melody's hand while he explained. "Not great-great-grandfather, just great-grandfather. Samuel was an old man when he moved back to New York with his young wife, and they had three boys. One of those boys was my grandfather. Between those three boys, there were another nine boys and five girls born, so it was a very prolific family. But why spoil an old man's appreciation of beauty with dusty old history?" Turning to Melody, "You are just as beautiful as LT said you were. It is a pleasure to meet you."

LT then moved on to the next two men. Both were introduced as bankers, and then a third man was identified as an oilman from Dallas. Bellamy brought everyone a fresh drink as the group sat and talked.

Melody was seated next to Abe Newhouse while LT and the other men talked oil, money, and the world economic climate. Abe turned to Melody. "LT and I have known each other for years. He's talked about you, but why have I never seen you? Is Texas so interesting you just couldn't leave?"

Melody demurred. "Well, I was in school until I finished my master's degree in history, then Mother was ill and I cared for her. After Mother passed, uh, well, I've just spent several months in England with the last of the English line of Farrs. I stayed in a place called Farr Cottage, and it's been in the Farr family since before the Norman Conquest. Fascinating history."

Abe took a small sip of wine. "Are you writing all of the Farr family history or just the Richard Farr in America part of the story?"

"Oh, I'm only writing certain parts of it. While I was in England, I began the Richard Farr saga. However, I met a man, Lord Alfred Oswin, who claims a kinship with my guardian, Lord Arthur Farr. I want to look into that and see what is there. In addition, while I've been home, I wrote some of the story of a child of Richard's, his daughter, Annis. Richard and Miss Lucy had twins, Avery and Annis, and I'm working on Annis right now."

"You have been busy! I suppose you will find many interesting things about your family. Any skeletons in the closets yet?"

Melody laughed. "No, but I think the Oswin-Farr relationship might have a few. It will be fun finding out if I am related to Alfred or not."

Abe noticed how she said Alfred's name. *Hmm, was there something there?* The conversations around the room stopped when Bellamy came to announce dinner. LT came, took Melody's arm, and led the group into the dining room.

Business talk ceased at the dinner table. LT told a couple of amusing stories about his first trip to New York many years before and how he was introduced to Abe. Everyone laughed and LT's stories were followed by the oilman from Dallas telling the group how he started in the oil business.

Bellamy silently moved around the room, serving and removing dishes as the dinner progressed. Each course was light, only a few bites of each dish, and the wine glasses were never more than a third full. The last item, a persimmon mousse with a whisky hard sauce, was the dessert which would leave everyone with a warm fall taste to savor as they enjoyed brandy and cigars on the terrace.

Melody took her brandy and sat where the cigar smoke would barley waft toward her. She liked the smell of cigars but not a barrage of smoke. Abe came and sat near her. "I don't smoke anymore, doctor's orders. I'm not supposed to drink anymore either, but, then, the doctor is my granddaughter, and so I listen to at least some of what she says. After all, I paid for her education, and I should get something out of it." He laughed. "Only a few of my children and grandchildren had any interest in going into banking. The rest, well, I'm happy none of them wanted to be lawyers."

Melody said, "As I was working on Richard Farr's story, I came across Samuel's granddaughter, Ruth, the one he brought to New York to marry off. However, there was nothing about her after that. Any idea what happened to her?"

Abe sipped his after-dinner drink. "You probably don't have anything about her in your letters because Samuel was very protective of her. Do you know the real reason he wanted to bring her to New York?" Melody shook her head. "He was afraid his granddaughter would marry a non-Jew, and his family here in New York couldn't have that. So he brought her here and she married. However, her husband was a very abusive man."

Melody looked shocked. "But couldn't Ruth's family, you know, uncles or cousins have done something about it?"

Abe shook his head. "No, you have to understand. At that time, the husband was the king of his house and no one from the wife's family would have dared interfere. Now, if it had been the husband's family, that would have been different, but they didn't. She lived a very mean life with him and died young. How she died," Abe shrugged, "nobody knows, but she was young."

Melody looked at her hands. Marriage was so chancy. She was sure Samuel Newhouse had believed the man he had married his granddaughter to was a good man. How was he to know what went on in another man's house and family? Melody's shyness about marriage seemed well-founded. LT's multiple marriages and the harsh life of Ruth; she didn't look forward to the prospect.

Abe could see the young lady thinking. He had spent enough years trying to read clients' thoughts he'd gotten fairly good at it, and this girl looked like she internalized things too much. He looked at his watch and decided it was time to go and leave her to her thoughts.

"Melody, I hope I see you again. Perhaps the next time you're in New York, you will do me the honor of letting me invite you to lunch. Any day but Saturday is good for me. I'm happy your god-father waited until after sundown before he had this little dinner party, or I would have missed meeting you." Abe shook Melody's proffered hand. "Humph, it's too bad you're not Jewish! I have a grandson who would make you a fine husband, but, well, LT will just have to arrange someone for you."

Melody blushed. "I'm afraid he is already looking. LT brought me to New York to get the dress for the charity ball. He wants to show me off in Houston. I wish people wouldn't try so hard."

Abe patted Melody's hand. "Don't turn down the help. Some of the longest-lasting marriages I know started with the help of family. Take care."

Melody waited until Abe had said his good nights to the rest of the group. One of the other men, a banker, also had to make it an early night, and the two men left together. LT and the last two guests finished their business, and Bellamy showed them out.

LT poured a whisky for himself and a scotch for Melody. "I think tonight was a great success, and your dress is simply amazing. Did you get that today?"

Melody nodded. "I'm glad you like it. It's one of my favorite colors, "Reagan Red." Mother had a coat this color and Father always said it marked her as a Reaganite long before it was fashionable."

"Well, it's late. I'm going to bed and sleep off all the eating and drinking we did tonight. What do you want to do tomorrow?" LT was just finishing his drink. He moved to put the empty glass on the bar.

Looking a bit surprised at the question, "Why, go to church of course! There is an Anglican church on the Upper East Side I want to visit. It belongs to the same convocation as our church in Houston. I asked Bellamy today to check the worship times and make arrangements to take me in the morning. And," she stifled a yawn, "you're right about it being time for bed. I'll never make it to church if I don't get some sleep. Good night, Pinky. See you in the morning!"

Louisa left for early mass at St. Patrick's, Pinky and Melody attended services at the church on the Upper East Side, and Mrs. Bellamy prepared to make brunch for everyone when they returned. Bellamy contacted an old friend from his time in the service and secured tickets for the 9/11 Memorial for everyone.

The brunch was, as always, amazing, and after it was over, two limousines took the group to the Memorial. Bellamy's buddy had been in the Pentagon on the day the plane crashed into the building and he was one of the guides at the 9/11 Memorial in New York.

Melody and LT stood and listened while the guide spoke. He talked about the exhibits, the memorial gifts that were still pouring in, the survivors of the Twin Towers, and the rescue workers on that day and for long after. The wall of photos of those who died made the impact of the victims and tremendous number of them very real. The pieces of rubble and the "slurry wall" from the site stood as gravestones for those who had perished.

LT, like the true gentleman he was, offered his handkerchief to a teary-eyed Melody. She had only been a teenager when the tragedy happened and it colored her life. Her graduate thesis at university had been on the history of terrorism prior to and including the attacks on September 11, 2001. The Memorial would now be a part of that ongoing memory.

Back in the hotel, LT received a message from one of the men who had been at the formal dinner the night before. The banker had a yacht at anchor in the Hudson River and wanted to know if the group would like a nighttime dinner aboard while they motored around the harbor. They would pass by the lighted Statue of Liberty, Battery Park, the Freedom Tower, and the famous skyline of New York. Everyone agreed it would be a fine end to a very moving day.

Early the following morning, the limousines took everyone back to the plane for the journey to Houston. New York receded from view and Melody was able to get a couple extra hours of sleep. LT, however, spent most of his time with a voice recorder dictating notes on his trip for his secretary, Marsha.

The cabin attendant, a very striking looking young woman in a starched black uniform, made sure everyone was awake before the plane landed in Houston. The West Houston Airport located close to the Energy Corridor was where the plane was based. The trip had been a domestic flight with no requirement for a customs or immigration officer, which meant there were no stops at Bush International Airport needed, and the plane could go right into its home base. LT's office had been alerted when the jet was about to land, and his driver was waiting for LT and Melody. Another driver and SUV took the luggage, the Bellamys, and Louisa to Melody's house.

LT wanted to see the results of the work Jose` and his crew had done while everyone had been in New York. Louisa left in her car, which had been parked at Melody's, and Bellamy brought in the luggage. Mrs. Bellamy, LT, and Melody looked first at the kitchen. The new cabinets were in, as well as the restaurant-grade appliances. The girls, Glen and Paul, had emptied everything from the kitchen and put it all back once the work was done. Mrs. Bellamy was very pleased with the changes. Melody and LT were amazed at the amount of work that had been done.

Melody and LT next checked the two rooms their lordships would be utilizing while they visited. The colors were neutral and muted, the furnishings were some Melody recognized from the attic or other rooms, and the floors and carpets had been freshly done. The baths for each room were also looking smart.

The last room was the suite Melody had chosen for herself, and she was a little apprehensive. A commotion in the hall and Mitzy's voice heralded the designer's arrival. LT and Melody waited for the reveal until Mitzy could join them.

"I don't mind telling you, getting these rooms ready for you in time was a bear! You are very lucky you have such wonderful contractors and extensive attics with lots of stuff from which to choose. However," Mitzy said with a smile and twinkle in her eye, "I did add some things which should up the wow factor. Behold," Mitzy said as she pushed open the doors, "Melody's grandmaster suite!"

LT gave a low whistle, and Melody stood in awe. She had never expected the room to look so polished and professionally done; well, at least not in the time they had given Mitzy to do the work. From the color on the walls, to the freshly cleaned Aubusson carpet under the bed, it all came together in a design that looked both warm and like Melody's private space. The bed from her old room was in the suite, but the rest of the items must had come from the Houston Design Center.

The group walked through to the sitting area and it was well coordinated with the bedroom to which it was attached. The bathroom and dressing room/closet she had chosen were also fresh and ready for the rest of Melody's things to be moved in.

As Melody opened some of the drawers in the bureaus in the dressing room, she noticed the maids had moved her things from her old room to the new. A glint caught her eye, and she looked to where a chaise lounge chair had been placed in the dressing room. Over the lounger, a small chandelier hung, and from the bottom of each light a string of crystals shone. Melody looked quizzically at Mitzy, "Crystals, really?"

"Hey girl, this is Texas, every girl's got to have some bling!"

Melody originally thought she would personally be busy making the food for Thanksgiving that she would be sending over to the church. Each year, the women and some men of the church cooked at home and brought pans of turkey, dressing, side dishes, pies, and more for the big Thanksgiving Day dinner. The doors opened at eleven in the morning and closed when the food was gone, usually about one or two.

In years past, Melody and her mother had spent the two or three days before the feast, baking pies, cakes, dressing, and turkey to take to the church, and then they stayed to serve those who came to eat. Everyone who ever participated got more out of it than the people they fed, and they got a whole heap. The ladies knitting circle always made hats, mittens, and scarves for the homeless. The children in Sunday school collected bottles of shampoo, soap, and toothbrushes to put in swag bags. The men made sure the families had other items that might be needed. No one ever left hungry or with empty hands.

This year, however, Mrs. Bellamy had taken over the cooking, and when Melody tried to help, was sent to the study to work on her family story. "Miss Melody, this is something I can do to help, plus Bellamy and I want to do it. Also, don't be surprised if Paul and Glen don't pitch in too. Mrs. LT was never interested in anything like this, and we are happy to do our part."

It wasn't until Melody saw the extent of the food that would be sent from her kitchen that she understood just how much was being done. It would all be greatly appreciated and enjoyed.

1905

Richard was shocked! Miss Lucy reached out to her daughter and tried to calm the waters. "Now, Annis, you have only just been introduced to young Mr. Lowell. It's much too soon to make that kind of declaration."

Calmly, Annis turned to her mother, "Oh Mother, don't worry. I know what I'm doing. Who else would I marry? He's perfect for me."

Richard had had about all he could take. "Miss Lucy, dear, please fetch the coats. I am sending the two of you home. I'll stay here and make arrangements with Avery and Greg Howard about the understanding between Greg's niece, Constance, and our son. I just don't know where this girl gets these ideas. Marry a boy she doesn't know? Ha! No she won't, and I don't want her here where he can bother her."

The Stuyvesant's maid brought the two ladies their coats, and the carriage was summoned by the butler. Chet Lowell tried to intervene, but Richard gave him a stern look and Chet's brother Hal pulled him away.

The atmosphere in the Farr house was tense for the next few days. Annis stayed in her room or the library. Then the entire family left the house to stay with Jeremy Higgins for a week while the workers came to electrify the house and install a telephone. Jeremy, Richard's old friend, mentor, and uncle by marriage to Miss Lucy, tried to mediate the problem but to no avail.

The only member of the Farr family who was not affected by the Annis/Chester problem was Avery. He loved his sister and wanted her to be happy, but his understanding with Miss Constance Howard was uppermost in his mind. The two families had agreed the match between Avery and Miss Howard was excellent and that there was a need for the young people to wait before marrying.

Avery would have to wait two years before he could ask Miss Constance to marry him. Richard was very adamant that Avery needed to work in New York learning the banking business before he could become engaged.

Samuel Newhouse was a very old man and had been partners with Richard when he first became a banker in Houston. Samuel had sold his share of the bank to Richard and moved back to New York in 1890 with his wife, Sarah, and their two young sons. Another son was born to Samuel and Sarah after the move, and all of his boys were working in the new bank Samuel had started in Manhattan. Unbeknownst to Richard, several more children also were born to the Newhouse family.

Richard and Samuel had remained friends through the years, and it was Samuel who was going to help young Avery as he worked in New York. A friend of Samuel's had a bank in Manhattan where Avery would spend his time learning all of the workings of a standard bank. However, when he was not busy in the financial district, he would be staying with Samuel's oldest son, Jacob, and learning at the Newhouse family's bank.

Samuel Newhouse was Jewish and in Houston had catered to the banking needs of the Jewish community. When he had taken Richard as a partner, the two men opened a standard bank with an office on the street for customers to use, but Samuel still remained the principal banker for his fellow Jews. In 1890, when he sold up to return to his native New York, Richard continued to serve Samuel's clients. For Richard, they were some of his best customers, and the Jewish community he served accepted and respected him.

Richard wanted Avery to have the same advantages he had enjoyed. The education in New York would give him the kind of cosmopolitan view Richard had learned in the bank in London where he first worked after Oxford and the education in banking Samuel Newhouse had imparted to him. Avery would be leaving at the end of August.

Annis, however, was another matter. No amount of patience, attempts at reasoning with her, or, in Miss Lucy's case, pleadings by her mother, could break through to her. The third evening of the Farr family's stay in the house of Jeremy Higgins was the turning point, well, partially.

After dinner, Jeremy invited Annis to take a walk with him in the garden. The tour through the flowerbeds laid down by Jeremy's late wife Abbey, did not last long, perhaps fifteen minutes, but when the two returned, Annis excused herself and went to bed. Jeremy said nothing about their conversation.

The next morning, however, Annis came to the breakfast table as almost the same person she had been before the party and the incident with Chester Lowell. She smiled, held conversations with her parents and others at the table, and even laughed at a funny story Avery told about his motor car. There was, though, something missing, and it escaped her parents what it might be.

On Friday afternoon, the Farr family moved back to their newly electrified house. In the main hallway, there was also a telephone that could be answered either in the butler's pantry or in the hall. It was customary for the butler or one of the servants to answer the phone, announce to the caller if the person they were calling was "at home," and then inform the family member who was being called of the need to speak on the phone.

When the family returned from church on Sunday, Mary opened the door to greet the head of the house. "Mr. Farr, a gentleman insists on seeing you. He wouldn't take no for an answer, and I put him in the library."

Richard Farr nodded and went straight to the library. A man of about his own age stood as he entered. He was tall like Richard but he had dark hair and dark eyes. Both men were about the same height, but the visitor had a more substantial mid-section than Richard.

"My name is Joseph Lowell, and I'm the father of Chester and Hector. My boy, Chet, uh Chester, is mooning around about some girl from a dance Chet and Hal went to a week or so ago. He says she is your daughter, and you have forbidden him to see her. Is that right?"

Richard motioned for the man to sit. "There is a bit more to the story than that I'm afraid. After having just been introduced to my daughter, Annis, your boy signed his name on every dance of her dance card. When I asked him about it, he proclaimed he was going to marry her. Such behavior is highly irregular and, in my mind, unbalanced. When I asked my daughter, she was equally unhinged, and that is when I sent her and her mother home. I did not want them anywhere near either of your boys."

Joseph Lowell sat on the edge of the chair. "Is my boy not good enough for your girl? He has just as much book learning as your Harvard boy and a good sight more than your daughter, I'll wager. His mother, my wife, was from one of the best families in New Orleans. And, even though I don't keep contact with my people back east, I am descended from the Lowells of Lowell, Massachusetts."

Richard put his hand up. "I don't doubt your boy is good enough, but it's the way he has tried to go about this. We don't know him, have never seen him except for this one social situation, and yet my daughter is telling me she is going to marry him and he is saying he is marrying her. Now what would you think of that if it was presented to you in this way? I know as the father of a girl, it is downright frightening!"

Joseph Lowell seemed to relax a bit. He looked around the room at the bookcases almost filled with books. Waving his hand to encompass the room, "Have you read all these?"

Richard looked surprised. "Why, yes, except for a few my wife and daughter have bought, yes, I have."

Mr. Lowell smiled. "Then, Mr. Farr, you must be a man with a very open mind and have a great imagination. Perhaps my boy didn't follow all the rules of society. His mother passed away when he and his twin, Hal, were just going into high school, and the college he went to was not as fancy as Harvard. But the boy has a good heart, is a hard worker, and for some reason, is entranced by your daughter. Do you think there might be some way for him to get to know you folks so you can judge him on more than a bad move at a party?"

Richard was wary. "Well, I don't know. Maybe, if he was to come to an "at home" one afternoon, but I would have to be here. He won't get to see Annis without either my wife or myself with her. They will be chaperoned."

Joseph Lowell chuckled. "I wouldn't want my boy to waste his time on any girl who wasn't carefully chaperoned. So when is the next "at home" he can come to?"

Richard sighed. "I suppose I should ask Miss Lucy, my wife. She is the one who keeps that particular social calendar." Richard got up and left the room. The family was in the sitting room, waiting for Richard to join them so they could have their Sunday lunch. He motioned for Miss Lucy to come to the settee in the hall.

Richard sat next to Miss Lucy and quietly said, "Joseph Lowell is in the library. I told him his boy could visit during one of your at homes and he wants to know when that would be."

Miss Lucy looked to Annis who was watching them intently. "If you think it's a good idea, this next Thursday, we will be at home from one to three. Do you think we should tell Annis?" She whispered back.

Richard looked at his little girl. Gone were the school uniform, the braids, and the ribbons in her hair. It was time he accepted the fact his sugar babe was a young woman. "Yes, sweetheart, I think we should. Perhaps," Richard looked at Miss Lucy and then to his daughter, "I want to introduce her to Joseph Lowell. He might as well get a chance to see what all the fuss is about."

Before Miss Lucy could agree or object, Richard had called Annis. "Sugar babe, there is someone here I suppose you should meet."

Annis got up and followed her father and mother to the library. The man who was waiting there stood as the ladies entered. Richard motioned to his wife. "Mr. Lowell, this is my wife, Miss Lucy, and this is my daughter, Annis." Then he motioned to the man standing in the room and said, "This is Joseph Lowell. He is Chester and Hector's father."

The only early spring flowers available were camellias but since they were one of Annis's favorites, they would do for the ceremony. Her beautiful blue dress, 'the butterfly,' which hadn't been worn since the night of the Stuyvesant's party, was altered to make it a lovely wedding gown. Long sleeves were added beneath the short ones of the party, and the neckline was adjusted to turn the dress from a gown for dancing to a wedding dress in which she would go to church and be married.

The courtship had lasted almost a full year, and from the beginning, everyone, whether they admitted it or not, knew it was only prolonging the time until marriage. Chet was always the perfect gentleman. Annis and Chet never tried to avoid Annis's parents or any chaperone they had designated as other young couples of the day were wont to do. The young couple, however, marked the days until they could wed.

St. John's Church was filled to capacity. The bride's side of the church wasn't big enough to hold all of the invited guests. However the side designated for the groom was almost empty, and her overflow sat on the Lowell side. Following the ceremony, the couple was feasted at Farr house. Chet and Annis Lowell stayed in Farr house on the first night of their married life and then left early the next morning on the train to New Orleans.

Chet Lowell's mother had been from New Orleans, and he wanted to introduce his bride to that part of his family. The couple stayed only three days in the city and then took the train to New York. A week in the big city with a chance to have dinner with Avery, Annis's twin brother, fulfilled all of the familial obligations. With only a few days left in their three-week honeymoon, the couple boarded the train for Detroit.

Shortly after the Stuyvesant's party, Richard Farr had concluded that automobiles were more than a passing fad. The 1905 Buick owned by George Place was the tipping point. Maude and George Place had given Avery and Annis a ride to the Stuyvesant's party, and before Richard had found the problem with the Lowell boys inside, he had joined the group of men who were admiring the car on the outside.

Richard's son, Avery, had owned an auto for the last year, but it seemed to Richard that Avery's car spent more time being repaired than being driven. The Buick and George's experience with it made Richard think more about the possibilities of having a car for himself. Shortly after the family's return from their stay with Jeremy Higgins, the idea of transitioning to a motor car was approached with the family.

Miss Lucy was very skeptical. She was more comfortable with the carriage and coachman. Avery and Annis were both very pro-motorcar. It was during these discussions on the family owning a motor that Avery and Annis revealed to their parents the fact

Annis was an accomplished driver. The revelation almost quashed the whole idea of the Farr family owning a car. It wasn't until Avery and Annis took their father for a drive in Avery's motor with Annis driving that the achievement was accepted.

The next step was to find out if the coachman, Frank Miller, would be able to handle both being a traditional coachman for Miss Lucy and a driver for Richard Farr. A few attempts with Avery's car were enough to convince Richard Farr of the need to hire someone who already knew both how to drive and how to maintain a motor car.

Mr. Jack Beetle was the owner of Beetle's Buick. Richard asked Jack to find him a qualified driver and someone who could take care of the car. The car Richard was buying, a 1905 Buick Touring Car, would need a professional driver. After several months, the car was delivered. A driver, Jimmy Jorgensen, who would fit the bill perfectly, came with it.

About the time Richard was taking his first ride in his own car with Jimmy at the wheel, Annis and Chet were in Detroit visiting a car manufacturing concern. The couple was not the only ones in the family who were in love with the new mode of transportation. Joseph, as well as Chet's twin, Hal, spent most of their spare time discussing, designing, and working on motorcars.

The Lowell farm was located between the Richmond Road and the Westheimer Road. At just over a thousand acres, it was not large enough for ranching on any kind of profitable scale, and Joseph Lowell wasn't really a dedicated farmer. The barns didn't contain any livestock but had been turned, instead, into mechanical shops where the men worked on cars, motors, and everything to do with automobiles.

The tour thorough the manufacturing facility was a revelation for Chet. He watched as the motors were built, the cars were crafted, and the various parts put together into a finished vehicle.

The owner of the company quizzed the young man and found him very knowledgeable.

Joseph Lowell's statement to Richard Farr that his boys might not have the fancy Harvard education Avery had did not mean they were uneducated. The twins had attended the Agricultural and Mechanical College of Texas at College Station in Texas (later to be known as Texas A&M). The oldest, and at the time, the largest university in Texas taught a classical education and with that education students could also study engineering. Joseph had attended the school when he was a young man and was one of the early alumni.

When the newlyweds boarded the train for the trip back to Houston, Chet and Annis both had new ideas about motorcars swirling in their heads. As Annis relaxed in Chet's strong embrace, the two discussed motors, drive trains, and chassis. At one stop, Annis got off the train to buy some sandwiches from a shop near the station, and Chet found a place where he could buy some pencils and a notebook. When the young couple were not sleeping or eating, they spent the time drawing sketches of what they had seen and exchanged ideas on things they thought would make intelligent changes in the designs.

Chet and Annis lived in the Lowell family home for the first year of their married life. A small cottage near the mechanical shops had originally been used for the workers when the farm/ranch was an agriculturally focused operation. Since the place was now empty, Annis asked to have it refurbished into a cozy place for the newlyweds to live.

The first time Chet had seen Annis was in the round barn on the Farr estate. She was wearing Avery's overalls over her riding skirt and shirtwaist, but now, she had her own overalls and simply wore underthings and a small-sized male "union-suit." Chet adored seeing his lovely wife, standing by his side with oil-stained work gloves protecting her delicate hands and working with him on a piece of machinery. Chet and Annis made a wonderful pair, both in their marriage and in the work they did together.

Joseph Lowell had built his first homemade automobile the year before the couple married, but he and his boys had been working on motors and other people's cars before that. The boys had each put together a car for their own use and with which to experiment. Early on, the Lowells wanted a place to run their creations. A large flat field near the shops was perfect. A long straight roadway was cut into it, tamped down with a steamroller, and turn-arounds cut at each end with a track leading back to the shop. A large oval was later cut in the same field that led to one end of the straightaway.

Almost three years into their marriage, on a Sunday afternoon, Chet and Annis were relaxing on the porch of the cottage. Chet was the first to hear it, a faraway mechanical noise; it was the sound of an engine but like the buzzing of a large mosquito. Almost instantly, Annis heard it also. The couple looked to the road near the property but saw nothing. The noise got louder, but it wasn't a smooth motor noise, something was wrong with it. A small dot in the sky got bigger and bigger until they realized it was an airplane.

The pilot barely made it to the end of the straight track near the shop. He bounced the plane a couple of times, then his engine cut out, and he rolled the length of the track and into the tall grass where he stopped. Joseph, Hal, Chet, and Annis were all there to help the man out of the aircraft. The man's name was Westerly, Jacob Westerly.

Jacob was shaken, but after a few minutes and a glass of cool water, he was able to express his surprise and thanks for the runway. "I was sure it was going to be some bumpy field with cows or gopher holes for me. My engine started making this terrible noise, and my life really did flash before my eyes."

Chet and Hal were already pulling the flying machine from the tall weeds back onto the hard-packed earth of the strip. Annis had gone to the shop to get one of the cars so they could pull the plane up to the shop where it might be repaired. Joseph had the cowling open over the engine, trying to see what the problem was.

The men and Annis spent the rest of that Sunday working on the plane. Jacob stayed and watched the work and towards evening, it was decided he would stay the night and leave the next day. Since the shop wasn't on the phone-line, Joseph took Jacob to the nearest telephone so he could call his family and let them know he was alright.

The next morning, the sky was clear, the plane was repaired, and Jacob wanted to pay his new friends for the work they had done on the engine of his airplane. More than anything, every one of the Lowells wanted a chance to ride in the plane. One by one, Jacob took them up for a short turn around the Lowell farm.

Joseph was especially taken by the view. The oval and straight-away that had been cut and steam-rolled into hard-packed surfaces gave him ideas for expansion. The two boys, Chet and Hal, in addition to Annis, fell in love with flying almost before the plane had left the ground. The trips ended too soon for them, but their futures in flying started in the small plane of Jacob Westerly. The Lowell Airpark came into being.

1915

Chet and Annis Lowell rarely made the trip to the Farr family home. Richard and Miss Lucy were still very active; and Avery had married his sweetheart, Constance, almost eight years earlier. Today, however, was special. Avery and Constance had produced a baby boy, Charles, and his christening in St. John's was a big event.

Charles Arthur Farr was welcomed into the Farr family like a prince. The church was full for the baptism, the buffet luncheon to celebrate rivaled a wedding reception, and the gifts ranged from silver cups, rattles, and combs, to a delicately carved ivory mobile to hang above his bed.

Richard and Miss Lucy no longer queried Annis and Chet about children. The young couple talked about nothing except planes, cars, and engines.

The oval track at the Lowell Airpark had been modified to allow for more speed. The straightaways had been lengthened and the curves banked to keep the fast cars from flying off. Hay bales lined both the inner and outer edges to help prevent injury. The airfield had also been improved. The original runway was lengthened; two more were installed with proper compass alignment and hangars built to accommodate the planes of the Lowell family and others who used the park.

The whole Lowell family was very proficient pilots. Chet and Annis often flew together, and the subject of racing had recently become a topic at dinner. Hal and Chet raced cars; they might as well race planes. An airplane race was being held in San Antonio the following weekend, and the Lowells were going to attend.

Chet and Joseph took off first, and the idea was to meet up over Sealy, Texas and follow the train tracks to San Antonio. A few minutes after the first plane took off, the second with Annis and Chet was powering up on the end of the runway.

Hal never could or would say why he had gone back to the airpark and made a pass to be sure the other plane took off on time, but he did. The runway was clear, and looking around the sky, no other plane was in sight. A puff of smoke from the field about a hundred yards off the end of the runway indicated there may be a fire. Banking to the left, Hal and his father looked for the source of the smoke and saw the plane Annis and Chet was in lying upside down with plumes of smoke rising from the tall grass around it. The large bird that had hit the plane on takeoff was dead and unnoticed in the undergrowth.

Hal landed the plane and taxied to the end of the runway closest to the downed plane. Both Hal and his dad were at the plane in seconds. Annis was easy to get out, but Chet was wedged into his seat. Annis was laid in the grass, and a small pickup from the shop arrived with a couple of the workers to see if they could help. Chet was finally taken out, and the husband and wife were placed in the back of the truck.

Hal took the wheel while his father knelt in the back with Annis and Chet. The closest doctor was three miles down the road and they arrived there as soon as possible.

The doctor looked first at Chet and pulled a blanket over him. Annis, however, was still alive. A quick exam told him she had internal injuries, a broken arm, and probably a broken hip. A call to the hospital was made, and the decision was to take her in the truck to the hospital. Moving her too much would only make matters worse than they were. The ten miles to the hospital was made with Annis lying, unconscious, next to her dead husband.

Hal called the Farr family as the gurney with Annis was being taken into surgery. A cousin, who Hal had called, took the body of Chet Lowell to the Lowell family home so he could be prepared for burial.

The two families, the Farrs and the Lowells, waited and prayed for the life of Annis. Richard and Miss Lucy called Dr. John Harris to consult with the doctor treating Annis, but he could not give much hope for a successful outcome. Joseph barely spoke to anyone, and the only person Hal talked to in more than single-word responses was Avery.

The attending doctor and John Harris came to the waiting area to talk to the families. "Her internal injuries are very extensive. Dr. Harris agrees they are beyond what we or anyone can do. I've given her something to lessen the pain and set the broken bones. She is being moved to a room and in about five minutes, you can all go in to see her. I wish I had better news, but the only physician who can help her now is the Great Physician, and each one of us needs to ask him for his help."

Annis' thoughts

I … I …where am I? Oh, it hurts! Why is Mother here? I can hear her voice, and that's Father. Why is Mother crying? Where is Chet? Oh, I am so sleepy. Hal, I know you're here, I can hear you. Where is Chet? Mr. Lowell? This isn't right! Why is everyone here, and … where is here?

Oh Chet! Oh I knew you would come. A vision of her husband appeared at the end of Annis's hospital bed. Dressed in his flight suit, he is holding the soft leather flying helmet he always wore in the open cockpit plane. *Why do you only stand at the foot of my bed? Why is everyone talking? Chet! Chet!*

Miss Lucy saw Annis trying to speak and took her hand. "Annis, Annis, honey, your Father and I are here. Oh my baby girl, please wake up!" As Miss Lucy spoke, the vision of Chet disappeared from the foot of Annis's bed. No one else saw him, only Annis.

Chet! Chet! Where are you? Don't leave me! As the vision of her husband, Chet, returned Annis relaxed. *Oh my love, please don't go again!* The voices of the people gathered in her room began to fade, and Chet stood silently, waiting to take his bride into his arms and into eternity.

Present day

To Melody's surprise, LT and young Mr. Higgins were at the church to help unload the food from the SUV that had come from Farr House. Everyone, including Gina, helped set up the food line and man the dessert tables. By one-thirty, the food had all been consumed, the desserts eaten, and the last knitted cap and scarf given out.

The parish hall was cleaned, everyone claimed their serving pans, and the people who had donated their time, talents, and food were all the richer for having provided Thanksgiving dinner to others who wouldn't have had such a meal. Now it was time to go home.

LT, Jeremy, Gina, and Melody had enjoyed some of the food served at the church and were not hungry. They were, however, anxious to catch some of the football games. The big screen in the media room at Farr House had been replaced before Melody's mother had passed away. Snacks, beverages, and plenty of seating for everyone in the house made for a really festive Thanksgiving.

The refrigerator in the kitchen, the one in the butler's pantry, and a spare in the bar were all stuffed with food. Melody gave all of the staff the rest of the day and the next three days off. However, having nowhere else to go and nothing else to do, the staff would still be in the house in case they were needed.

Melody had made a special pumpkin pie. Later in the evening, she and Gina slipped away to the kitchen to make the whipped cream to go with it. A very spicy pumpkin pie made with dark rum and black molasses had been her father's favorite. The whipped cream, in addition to having vanilla flavor in it, also had a shot of light rum to go with the pie. Her mother had taught her to make it just as Melody's grandmother had taught her mother. The recipe originated from a freed slave employed by Richard and Miss Lucy after they first married and was a standard for Thanksgiving and Christmas.

Mrs. Bellamy watched as the whipped cream was made. She had written down the recipe when Melody made the pie, and now she wanted to make sure she had the rest of the dessert for her kitchen books. Melody then insisted Mrs. Bellamy go sit with the others while Melody and Gina served everyone.

The game everyone was watching was in half-time, and the pie was especially well received. Jeremy and LT both liked the kick of the rum, and it was fortunate that Melody had made two pies and plenty of whipped cream. By the end of the half time show, the pies and topping were gone.

The staff started to drift away to their own quarters, Gina left to get home while she was still sober enough to drive, and LT poured a last round of drinks for himself, Jeremy, and Melody. ESPN finished the final rundown on the day's games, and LT called his driver to come pick them up.

Jeremy helped Melody take the things from the media room, put things away, and place dishes in one of the dishwashers. In no time, the kitchen was clean, the last chip and drink cleared, and the driver had buzzed the gate to be let in. LT and Jeremy said their goodbyes and Melody went off to bed. It had been a very long, happy day.

Early the next morning, Melody was awakened by the familiar IM *ping* of her computer. Alfred was on the net and wanted to talk. Melody went to her desk and asked for ten minutes to wake up, and then she would love to IM with Alfred.

Almost twenty minutes later, Melody was on the net with Alfred. She apologized for being late, and Melody explained to him that she had given the staff three days off. However, when she went to the kitchen to get her coffee, she found all of them up, breakfasted, and preparing to put up Christmas decorations in the house. No amount of cajoling could get them to relax, so the decorations were going up anyway.

Jose` and one of his brothers had brought a couple of their men to put the lights up outside and to raise the chandelier in the foyer high enough to get the tree positioned under it. When she left to do the IM with Alfred, Bellamy was putting the two six-foot nutcrackers outside on either side of the front door.

Alfred and Melody chatted for more than an hour before they signed off. Alfred did tell her the travel plans had changed. Instead of Alfred and Arthur arriving on Tuesday of the next week, they would arrive on Wednesday. A friend of LT's was flying from Vienna to Houston. The friend's business jet would be stopping in south London at the Biggin Hill Airport in Bromley. Arrangements were made for their lordships to travel via the friend's private jet.

Melody made a mental note to ask LT about the changes, but she wanted to see what the staff was doing with the decorations.

Gina arrived just before lunch, and LT brought Jeremy to pitch in also. Mrs. Bellamy wanted to make lunch for everyone, but LT insisted on doing the honors. With refrigerators full of food, he had a lot from which to choose. He made a call to his driver to pick up fresh bread from the bakery, and later, lunch was set out buffet style in the kitchen and morning room.

Thin slices of turkey, brioche, lettuce, tomato, and the most important for Melody, mustard and Miracle Whip made wonderful turkey sandwiches. Mrs. Bellamy's roughly-cut coleslaw was just the right side to go with the meal. Between the staff, Jose`s' workers, and the visitors, it made a lovely feast and a much-needed time-out for rest. All thanked LT for the lunch.

The decorations were completed, except for a few items Melody wanted to get from the florist, by the middle of the afternoon. Gina stayed to visit, and LT took Jeremy to visit a distant cousin who lived near Rice University.

Gina and Melody hadn't spent much time together the last week or so, and it was time to catch up. The young man Gina had met at LT's final barbecue was escorting her to the charity ball the next weekend. Melody wanted to show Gina her dress but had decided to keep it a secret from everyone, even Gina, until the night of the event.

LT had asked her what color the dress was and had even wanted to see it after it arrived and Louisa had finished altering it. All Melody would tell him was that it was blue. That seemed to satisfy him, and Melody hadn't thought any more about it until she and Gina had gotten together and talked about dresses.

Gina fell in love with the gorgeous red, Reagan Red, dress Melody had bought in New York. Both girls had about the same coloring and it would have been perfect on Gina but not as much so as on Melody. Gina was wearing a deep rose dress with a bolero jacket trimmed with seed pearls of the same hue. The look would be stunning, and Gina couldn't wait to wear it.

By that evening, everyone had gone home or out to a movie and dinner. It surprised Melody when the buzzer from the front gate sounded. Bellamy answered and it was LT.

Bellamy put LT in the study and called to Melody on the intercom. LT looked like a schoolboy who had a secret that just wouldn't keep. In his hands, he held a flat velvet box.

"I hope you don't mind me coming by so late, but I was on my way home and wanted to bring this to you. Someday, I will take you to the vault where the jewelry you inherited is kept, but since you have a blue dress, I thought you might like to wear this to the charity ball on Saturday." LT opened the lid of the box, and a beautiful gold filigree necklace with sapphires and diamonds was displayed within. A pair of identical earrings was also included.

"My, my!" Melody exclaimed. "Richard gave this necklace to Miss Lucy from some of the profits from the oil money. Miss Lucy let Annis wear it for her coming-out party. Oh, it will go perfect with my dress. Thank you!" Melody hugged LT and he blushed.

"Aw, it's stuff like this that should be used. You own it, you might was well wear it! Look, I can't stay. The car is outside and I need to get some sleep. How about getting dinner tomorrow with Jeremy and me?" Melody nodded, and LT left to get home.

Dinner at the St. Charles Club was always something Melody anticipated with delight. She had taken the red dress from New York out the day before to show Gina and decided the dress would get its first public outing at dinner. A pair of silver sling-back pumps and a beaded bag was all she needed.

The weather was starting to turn in Houston. Natives always joked about the "three weeks of winter," but that didn't mean the nights were not like fall in late November, or early in December. Her mother had a couple of coats that might have been suitable, but her grandmother had an opera cape that looked great with the dress. However, Melody just wasn't ready to go the cape route yet and opted for a faux fur stole of her mom's.

LT was the only one to get out of his limo when he and Jeremy came to pick Melody up for dinner. At the club, LT put Melody's stole in the checkroom and turned to catch the look on Jeremy's face when he first saw Melody in the red dress. LT smiled to himself. Maybe there was a possibility there after all.

All of the background checks, financial assessments, and discussions with people who knew Jeremy showed him to be a fine, upstanding man. LT had spent several hours with the man, talking and getting to know him, but there was one part of him he kept quiet about. That was his immediate family. He just didn't say anything about his parents or grandparents. The file on him mentioned an older cousin, George, who ran the family business much like LT ran the holding company for his extended family. However, Jeremy's family wasn't as vast or into as many businesses or properties as the Chadwick Holding Company was.

The service at dinner was as flawless as always; the food, wine, and all that went with it were equally impeccable. LT invited

Melody back to the apartment for coffee and brandy. He knew she had given her staff the whole weekend off and didn't want to intrude, but she declined.

"LT, I am going to church tomorrow, so I want a clear head and plenty of sleep. It wouldn't be nice to nod off during the sermon." Jeremy walked her to the door, and Bellamy was there to open it for her.

On Sunday, LT and Jeremy were in church but left just after the service to watch the football games at a cousin's house. Gina and Melody got a salad at the Salad Hut, but Gina had to work on a presentation she was giving to investors on Monday. Melody was left alone the rest of the day with the family history.

She had just started to put the things away from the time period she had been working on when she received a call from LT. A glance at her watch told her it was almost six in the evening.

"Hey, girl, Jeremy and I are hungry and wondered if we, or rather, I could use your barbecue pit? We have just sat through some of the most disappointing games of the season and meat on the grill, good company, and some of those leftovers you have in the fridges at your house would be a treat. Does that sound good to you?"

Melody laughed. "Sure. If I eat any more turkey before Christmas I'll start growing feathers. Come on over."

In less than half an hour, the men arrived with a couple grocery bags, and Jeremy had a case of beer. Mrs. Bellamy came out to see who was in her kitchen, but Melody and LT both sent her and Bellamy back to their day off.

"This next week is going to be busy enough," Melody reminded them, "so take the time, and if you are hungry, it looks like LT has brought enough to feed an army. I'll let you know when the meat is ready."

Before LT stepped out to get his grill fire started, he had an order for Jeremy and Melody. "I've got this. I can handle dinner; you two just have a drink and wait for the food."

Jeremy grabbed a beer and put the rest of the case in the drink fridge under the bar. Melody took a bottle of water and the pair joined LT in the back lanai. The Texas night was crisp and cool, but a fire in the outdoor fire-pit was enough for them to be comfortable with just their jackets.

LT looked over at the young couple. He liked young Jeremy. A match between him and Melody would be good for her and for the future of the legacy her great-great-grandfather had left her. True, the Marine still had a few years left on his "20," but Jeremy hadn't indicated if he intended on staying in until he could retire. He didn't need the money. His family money, although small in comparison to Melody's fortune, would be plenty for anyone to live on comfortably.

Melody sipped her water. "So, Jeremy Higgins, how do you like Houston?"

Jeremy set his bottle on the table that was between them. "Oh, it's OK. It's a lot bigger than most places I've been, but at least here, in this house, it seems far, far away. Yep, it's nice here and at LT's place."

Turning to Jeremy, Melody thought it was time she asked him a question she had been dying to ask. "You know, every time we are around each other, you talk about people in your grandparents family and older but never your family. Do you mind if I ask you about your family?"

Jeremy frowned, "There's not much to tell, but I'll make you a deal. You answer a question for me and I'll answer yours. But," before she could ask her question, "I get to ask first. Deal?"

Melody nodded. "Ask away. I can't think of anything I wouldn't answer."

"Well, you are the family, or at least this family's keeper of their history and I know it intersects with my family. That day I met you in the churchyard, in the cemetery, I asked you about my namesake." Melody nodded and Jeremy went on, "Do you know how he died?"

"Sure, I was just going over some of the journals, letters, and diaries of people in my family from that time period. He was my great-great-grandmother's uncle by marriage, but he was also the best friend and mentor of Richard Farr, my great-great-grandfather. This is what I know about it."

1906

The house seemed so empty to Miss Lucy and Richard. Annis and Chet were on their honeymoon, Avery was in New York working in a bank, and it would be a year before Avery and Miss Howard would be marrying.

Their old friend Jeremy Higgins called almost every evening. Jeremy had lost his wife Abbey almost two years before, and even though one of his young grandsons had moved into the house with him to keep him company, the boy's little children made an awful racket. He knew that in Richard's house he could have some adult conversation, good food, and no interference from crying babies or toddlers with sticky fingers. Being a grandpa and great-grandpa was wonderful but not full-time!

Jeremy still rode his horse to the house. Others were getting motorcars, even his grandson had one, but Jeremy couldn't give up his old horse.

While Annis and Chet were in Detroit marveling at the future of transportation, Richard and Jeremy were sitting on the side porch talking about ranch life and how it was disappearing. The sun was setting with beautiful hues of blue, gold, red, and yellow. Jeremy set his glass of bourbon on the side table, closed his eyes, and drifted off to sleep. Richard asked the butler to bring a lap robe for Jeremy so he didn't catch cold, but Jeremy had passed away. He and his Abbey were reunited. Age, Jeremy was in his late eighties, and missing his Abbey had finally caught up to him.

Three days later, the funeral was held at St. John's Church. All the time Jeremy had been laid out in the front parlor of his home, guests streamed in. Men and women in silks and linens or others in boots, jeans, and Stetsons, city and country, they all came to pay their respects to the family of Jeremy Higgins. A pile of telegrams arrived from friends, fellow ranchers, and politicians in Washington as well as Austin, current and retired. The governor sent his son as his representative at the burial.

The local papers carried obituaries and one of the New York papers even talked about the "end of an era" of cattle, oil, and big men with big dreams. For Richard and Miss Lucy, he was family. Richard had already mourned one father when he was a young man just starting his life, and Jeremy stepped in to help steer him along as a father would through marriage, children, and beyond. Now, Richard's second father was also gone, and the quiet ticking of the passing years began to grow louder.

On the day of the funeral, it rained. Richard looked around at the people gathered in the little churchyard. A sea of black blocked out the green spring grass. The heavy gray of the skies; closed off the earth to the warmth of the sun; it was the perfect weather for a funeral. As the Anglican priest intoned the funeral service, Richard thought no one should be buried on a warm spring day with flowers blooming, birds singing, or children playing. No. Death should not be associated with something so sweet, only with darkness and sadness. The day of Jeremy's funeral was just that kind of dark day.

end

"Hmm, you're a good storyteller. I'll pass the information on to my aunt. She always wants to know about our family, and this is another item I am sure she'll love."

Melody looked at Jeremy. "Ok, I answered your question. Now what about mine?"

Jeremy grinned, "Fair's fair. What do you want to know?"

"I want to know about your family, your parents, if you have any brothers or sisters, growing up; that kind of thing. You never talk about them, and, well, you know about me, what about you?"

"Hmm, OK, but there really isn't much to tell. No brothers or sisters. I lived with my grandparents, went to college, joined the Marines, end of story."

"No, no, no. You don't get off that easy." Melody insisted.

Jeremy could see by the set of her shoulders and the look in Melody's eyes that she was determined to get him to talk. "Alright, but it's pretty boring."

Jeremy's story

"I lived with my grandparents from the time I was seven. They were great, but it would have been nice if I could have lived with my parents. You see, just after my seventh birthday, Mom and Dad wanted to go to some kind of family thing in Carmel, California. Mother was from Carmel. Normally, they would have flown out on a commercial flight, but the airlines were grounded because of a strike."

"My father was a pilot. In fact, he got his pilot's license before he got his driver's license. Mother never got one, but she had done the ground school. Dad would let her take the controls sometimes, but she would do the radios and maps for him so they were kind of a team. Dad was instrument rated, but he would never go over the mountains. This time, however, they decided to take the southern route and fly through a pass or something to get across the Rockies to the West Coast."

"I remember them talking about the route. They planned for two days, bought some oxygen for the plane in case they had to go too high, and then they checked the whole thing with my grandparents. Both of them were pilots, so I guess it was all OK."

"Gran took us to the airport so I could say good-bye to them. Usually, I would have gone with Mother and Father, but the school year had just gotten underway, and they didn't want me to miss the two weeks they would be gone. That was the last I saw of them."

"They called, well, Mom called almost every night while they were gone, and when the two weeks was up, they started on the return trip. Granddad said the weather was perfect all the way home, and he took me to the airport to watch them land. We waited and waited. Granddad kept me busy looking at planes, showing me stuff in the hangars, and the longer it got, the harder he tried to make it seem everything was OK."

"About two hours went by, and he started questioning somebody about the check-in points for the flight plan they had filed. One of the stations stated they had not reported in when they should have. The airport continued to call the plane but did not receive any response. Granddad telephoned the last place they had reported, and then he called Gran to come and get me."

"I went back to my grandparent's house while Granddad tried to find out what was going on. He was sure they had landed and gone to a motel to spend the night and just hadn't suspended the flight plan. It would have been unusual for them to do that but not beyond the realm of possibility. I stayed with Gran while Granddad called every airport listed between the last check-in and the one they had missed. Finally, the authorities declared the plane missing and initiated a search."

"That was a little over twenty-five years ago, and nothing was ever found. No wreckage, nothing. Even when the official search was called off, Granddad paid some people to keep looking, but they had just disappeared."

End of Jeremy's story

"That's terrible! At least you had your grandparents, but still, I can't think what it would have been not to have had my mother and father. That must have been hard on you."

Jeremy nodded. "It was, but I think the hardest was the way my cousin George acted. He used to tease me when I was growing up that my parents had simply left. Left me, left our home, just took the plane and flown down to Mexico or Central America. Humph, I used to get in trouble for trying to beat him up over that. He was bigger, so I was the one who came off the worse for it. But that didn't mean I didn't try."

Melody grinned. "No wonder you don't have a very close relationship with your cousins. Were they all like that or just George?"

"Let's just say they didn't dispute what he said, but the day I first came home in my uniform, George kind of apologized for being such a rat when we were kids. Something about the "eagle, globe, and anchor" convinced him it was time to call a truce."

Jeremy looked around and back at Melody. "So do you mind another question? It's not personal, but…"

Melody grinned. "Ask away!"

"This house, it looks too new to be the one your great-great-grandfather built. What happened to the original one or was this one just renovated to look like an Italian villa?"

LT interjected. "The food's ready, so let's go in and eat. I want to hear about the house myself so," turning to Melody, "you can include me in the storytelling."

"I would love to tell both of you. Some of it my father used to tell me, but the diary of Miss Lucy's that I found in Grandmother's room has added a lot he never mentioned."

1915 – The Storm

August was unusually hot for Houston. The air seemed oppressive; the humidity made the prospect of moving from one room to the other a chore, and little Charles Farr was sitting with Nanny Wilson in the summerhouse. The screens kept the bugs out, a ceiling fan moved the air, and a strengthening breeze promised some relief from the heat.

The Farr family had several men working in the gardens. Mrs. Avery had ideas about making an Italian garden like one they had seen on their honeymoon travels several years before. The palazzo where they stayed impressed the young couple, and the workmen were there to try to make her vision a reality at her home.

One of the men, however, was not working, but spent his time looking at the sky. At first nanny supposed he was just being lazy or perhaps he was supposed to watch for rain, but when a foreman came and started making angry gestures at him, the man calmed him and pointed to the sky. Both men were looking up and gesturing to the other men.

Johnny B., the man who was watching the sky instead of working, had survived the hurricane that had devastated Galveston, Texas, in 1900. He was an orphanage boy. He lived his whole young life in the orphanage on Galveston Island until a week before the storm. A family came from the mainland to see about adopting a boy, and unlike the other times when he and his friends were disappointed to be left behind, he was the one chosen to leave with a family.

The family he went with had a small farm about twenty miles north of Galveston on the outskirts of Houston. He was just getting settled in, learning what chores he would have to do, and trying hard not to miss his friends when the worst happened. He was out in the barnyard taking feed to the hogs when the woman of the family called him to come back into the house. The man and their own son came in just behind him. They started taking things from the kitchen, blankets and pillows from the beds, and any extra clothes they might have.

The barn had a cellar dug into the floor with stones lining the walls. It was cool, dark, and damp. The walls were lined with shelves containing rows of canned goods and a couple of fifty-gallon glazed stone crocks positioned in the corner. The food items from the kitchen joined the canned goods; a basket of vegetables was put in one of the stone crocks with other root tubers. Four stools were brought down, and planks were put across them for bedding and pillows.

The rest of the day, the stock was taken to the field and allowed to graze; the pigs and chickens were fed and moved to the north side of the barn. Off and on bands of rain and wind, sometimes very heavy, raced across the sky. However, it was when the sky turned a sickly yellow, any remaining birds flew off toward the north, and the other farm animals paused and waited for what was to come…

To the south, a wall of clouds from the earth up to heaven was moving toward them. The clouds churned, lightning flashed and bolted within them, and the wind started to pick up in earnest. The man told everyone to get into the cellar. He checked the last few things around the house and barn, and then he also got into the cellar and secured the trapdoor closed with a heavy piece of wood. The woman lit a candle from a tin box where they were stored. She had baked that morning so there were fresh bread loves, some cheese, and the remains of a pie from the day before.

In the night, the storm hit. The chinks between the boards of the trapdoor allowed for the sound to enter, and it was frightening. The roar began and didn't let up. It seemed like hours passed, and the storm continued to pound. Other noises ... the banging of a barn door, screams from the pigs, the breaking of the glass in a window of the barn, were all faint compared to the sound of the storm.

The flicker of the candle and the draw of the smoke through the trapdoor heralded the shift in the winds. The monster storm was moving past, but the sounds of the wind kept them trapped in their hole. Sometime the next day, or was it the day after that, they finally came out of the cellar.

It was still raining, the wind was still high, but the majority of the storm was past. It would take several weeks to fix all the damage, but getting the stock in from the pasture and looking after the pigs and chickens was a top priority. A couple of the chickens were dead and a pig was speared with a large wooden splinter, but the farm had fared better than most.

Johnny B. was at the local store with the man a few days after the storm getting some supplies. A picture in the window, cut from the Houston paper, caught his eye. In black and white, the photo would haunt him forever. It was a picture of the orphanage in Galveston where he had lived. It was in ruins, many of the children and staff were killed along with people from Galveston in the worst recorded hurricane ever to hit the United States. What upset Johnny B. was the child he could make out in the photo; it was his friend, Billy. He was one of the boys not picked a few days earlier to go home with a family. Now, Billy and probably all of their friends were dead.

The sky that day over the Farr estate looked very much like the sky before the Great Storm of 1900. Johnny B.'s foreman, a man who had also lived through the remnants of the Storm as it passed north of Houston, agreed the sky was more threatening than a summer thunderstorm. The foreman left to tell his boss.

The staff as well as the workers who were building the gardens, were put to work on securing the house and grounds against the approaching hurricane. Richard and Avery came home from the bank while Constance and Miss Lucy supervised the packing of books, silver, china, and crystal to be put in the round barn. Richard had always said the round barn was the most storm-worthy building on the estate. It had survived several tornados and the Great Storm of 1900; it would survive this storm also.

The workers were sent home to care for their families and the Farr family and staff went into Richard's study. The original builder of the house was no longer alive, and Richard doubted the workers who helped construct the house would even remember the extra care that had gone into building the study. Richard was a banker, and it was not unusual for him to have a sum of money or valuables in the house. Two large safes had been installed in the study to keep these items. The paneling that covered them matched so well that the door to the niches which held the safes was hard to find if a person didn't know they existed. The entire study had double walls, a fact that was not apparent to the casual viewer and the people who lived in the house never felt the room was any smaller than the outside measurements of the adjoining rooms would indicate. What Richard had built was a safe room.

The household was hunkered down when the hurricane hit. One of the maids, a girl named Jane, screamed when the sound of glass breaking filtered into the study, but mostly, the sound was the dull roar of the wind. The hurricane came in waves. Richard knew it was the outer bands of the storm that were hitting the house, and the main hurricane was still coming.

The house had fared quite well during the Great Storm of 1900. The main body of the hurricane was far enough to the east that the only damage was to the roof of the stables and some of the tiles from the roof of the main house. A couple of trees also came down. Richard was sure this storm wouldn't be any worse than the earlier one at the turn of the century.

Richard was proved wrong in his assessment when the hurricane hit to the west of Farr House, putting them on the *dirty* side or dangerous side of the storm. The roar of the winds was punctuated by the constant sounds of shattering glass and breaking timbers. The house was being torn apart. The square building Richard had thought so highly of when he had visited his friend during his university years was wonderful in the English countryside. However, it was not appropriate on the Gulf Coast of Texas when it was hurricane season.

The storm tore at the sharp corners and lifted up the roof. Debris and pieces of trees crashed through windows, and rain blew through in sheets. The house would be a total loss, except for the study. Richard had it carefully built to protect valuables from the bank. On this day, however, it also protected his most precious valuables, his family and servants.

As the family came out of the room, the sun shone from a clear blue sky. All around were the remains of the house, the stables were in a shambles, and the only thing standing was the round barn.

Richard and Avery packed their families off to Jeremy Higgins's old house. The place had set empty for a couple of years when the grandson had won a seat in the US Congress and moved his family to Washington. Richard had promised to look after it, and the old stone structure was still as sound as the day it was built.

As Richard and Avery gathered men to clear the debris, plans for a new house were whirling in Avery's head. When he and Constance Howard had married, he had taken her on a long trip to Europe. She loved the place they stayed in Italy, and it was the villa where they spent two weeks that impressed Avery the most. He talked to his father about it, and Richard agreed. Avery and his son, Charles, were the future of the family, so Richard would like Avery to have the kind of design he preferred.

It took almost eighteen months to complete the house, but it was worth the wait. Constance and Miss Lucy accompanied Richard on a trip to New York where several of the pieces of furniture were either purchased and shipped or sketches made and the items fabricated in Houston by local craftsmen. The dining room table, however, was shipped from England. It was an inlaid work of art, and the matching chairs, sideboards, and cabinets became the focal point of the huge room.

Constance might have loved the Italian villa design, but her taste in furniture was very eclectic. Some of the rooms were the modern Art Deco, others Victorian, and one sitting room was a mix of Second Empire and very early Victorian. Somehow, though, it all worked, and the family liked it. The secrets the surviving study held stayed with Richard, who passed them to Avery, who told them to Melody's father when he was a young boy. They were, however, still to be revealed to Melody.

end

LT chuckled. "And they will not be revealed to Melody until her wedding or she reaches the majority under her father's will. He was very insistent on that point." Melody frowned at her father's best friend who continued, "And don't look at me like that. I certainly don't know them. It's all in some documents he left in the bank's safe." Then faking a mysterious pose, "Just wait and all will be revealed!"

The last bit broke the mood. Melody laughed and directed her comment to Jeremy. "You see what I have to put up with?"

Jeremy patted her hand, "Sometimes there are things that are too important in a family to leave to the whims of youth. I'm sure your father had good reason to arrange his will the way he did. If you had seen some of the things I have, you would be happy to be so protected, but that conversation is for another night." Looking over to LT, "Don't you have some early meetings in the morning? I'm ready to hit the rack."

LT nodded to his young friend, pulled his cell phone out, punched in some numbers, and turned to Melody. "It should only take a few minutes for the car to come. Thank you for the use of your barbecue. It's been a few weeks, and I guess I was having some withdrawal symptoms. I miss my grill at the house."

"So," motioning to Jeremy, "let's put the plates in the dishwasher for Melody and toddle off to my place for a good night's sleep."

Melody laughed at the idea of the men doing the dishes. "Please, let me do that. I think enough beer and whisky has been consumed tonight. The dishes don't need to take the punishment!" Before LT's driver buzzed the front gate, Melody had put away the things from the table, the dishes went into the dishwasher, and the empty bottles into the recycle bin. "See, all done!"

After seeing her guests to their car, Melody set the alarm and went off to bed.

Less than a minute later, Bellamy checked the house, made sure the alarm was activated, and smiled. His employer had retired for the night, and now, he could also.

The next few days were very busy. The remaining few decorations were put up for Christmas, the final touches were finished in the two rooms their lordships would occupy during their stay, and an extra employee was added to the staff on a temporary basis.

Bellamy had suggested and LT had agreed that a manservant, who would take care of the two English guests, should be engaged. On Monday afternoon, Robert Latrell, or simply Robert, arrived. The servant's quarters on the third floor hadn't seen any occupants since the time of Melody's grandmother, but now it was fortunate to have the extra room.

In addition to attending to Lord Alfred and Lord Arthur, Bellamy wanted Robert to assist in serving during meals, making drinks, and helping with the parties that had been scheduled. Melody had discussed it with LT, and in addition to the Christmas party, the New Year's Eve celebration, and the charity ball, two dinner parties had been planned. It would be a busy December, and the addition of Robert to the staff, even temporarily, would lessen the weight on the others.

When Avery Farr had commissioned the rebuilding of Farr House after the storm of 1915, he engaged a builder who employed a family of Italian stonecutters. It was this group of men who laid the marble and granite floors, cut the tiles for the bathrooms, but most importantly, cut and laid the stone of the house itself. Farr House would never again be destroyed by hurricane or even by tornado.

The limousine LT had sent to pick up the English visitors had just turned off the street and come up to the gate of Farr House. Alfred and Arthur, sitting in the rear seat, could see the small plaques on each gatepost with the inscription Farr House. What was probably even more stunning was the dragon, fashioned in wrought iron, which adorned the gate.

Alfred was the first to see it and he nudged Arthur with an elbow. "Isn't that the dragon from your family's crest? Fancy putting it on a gate!" Arthur's only response was to shake his head.

The gate opened at the driver's request to the house, and the vehicle moved slowly forward. LT's instructions to the driver had been specific. "Maximum effect, Mike, maximum effect. Oh, and make sure you bring them at the best time to catch the sun, about four or so should be just about right." The timing was perfect.

The driveway to the house was not a straight, short drive, but had been purposely designed to curve with the fall of the land. The first view their lordships had of Farr House was intended to be outstanding, and it succeeded. The sun hit the tiny flecks of quartz in the stone that had been used to construct the house, and they shone brightly, seemingly with a light of their own. The size and magnificence of the building, as well as the design, fashioned after an Italian palazzo, was meant to impress, and it did.

Neither man spoke, but both began to understand one simple fact: Melody Farr was neither plain nor a pauper. The mystery of her father's will was all but explained. LT's driver, Mike, pulled up to the front door where the staff stood along with Melody, LT, and Jeremy.

Bellamy and Robert opened the car doors and returned to the staff line. Melody walked forward to greet her guests.

"Welcome to Farr House!" She hugged and kissed Arthur first then Alfred on the cheek before releasing them to introduce the staff. "Bellamy is my house manager/butler, Mrs. Bellamy the cook, Robert has been engaged to see to both your needs, and the maids, Pauline and Glenda, also known as Paul and Glen. Everyone is here to see that you enjoy your visit."

As she steered her guests up the steps to the front door, she came to LT and Jeremy. "LT Chadwick was my father's best friend and my trustee. We just call him LT, and this is Jeremy Higgins, the great-great-grandnephew of Richard Farr's best friend and mentor. He is staying with LT for an extended leave."

Arthur and Alfred exchanged a glance. So, Jeremy might be competition for Melody's affections, and LT was probably favoring him. The two men smiled. Breeding and having been raised the way they were guaranteed nothing would show on their faces.

Alfred didn't know if Arthur had gotten the jab yet, but the greeting Melody was giving them was so very, very different from the greeting she had received at Farr Cottage in England. Inwardly, it made Alfred smile.

Alfred and Arthur moved inside with Melody and her other guests while the staff got the bags from the trunk of the car. Bellamy and Mike, however, had a different mission. The doors to the back seat were still open, and Bellamy noticed the opened bottles of water in the holders. Mike carefully handed each bottle to Bellamy who bagged and tagged each bottle.

Bellamy nodded as he handed the plastic bags with the bottles in them back to Mike, "Thanks, Mike. Just give these to Rodney in the security office. He knows what to do with them. Mr. LT and Jeremy won't need you again until after dinner sometime, but as always, I'll call when they are ready to leave."

As Bellamy entered the house and closed the door, he caught Mr. LT's eye and gave him a slight nod. LT chuckled to himself. It would take a few days, but the DNA tests on the two men would solve the mystery and ongoing argument between their lordships of who was related to whom. It was his job to look after Melody's interests and knowing who was who. Information was simply another tool.

Shall We Dance?

inner on the first evening was low-key. Alfred and Arthur had been up for several hours and even though jet lag would not begin to affect them until at least the next day or two, they would want to sleep early. Drinks in the lounge, a lite meal in the dining room, and coffee with brandy in the lounge after dinner was finished and their lordships were in bed before nine. Melody promised them a tour of the house the next day.

Melody was usually an early riser, but Arthur and Alfred were still running on GMT which made her early look late to her guests. Mrs. Bellamy put out generous plates of sausages, grilled tomatoes, eggs, bacon, and kept the toast rack full. Bellamy and Robert kept the coffee, tea, and orange juice glasses topped off.

Alfred left the table for a few minutes, and his absence gave Arthur a chance to talk to his ward alone. "I see now why you were going to be late getting back to us. This house and the staff are almost a full-time occupation for you. Have you done anything on the family history you were anxious to complete?"

"Oh, I've done quite a bit, but you shouldn't think all of this" waving her hand to encompass the whole room, "was anything like what I came home to when I left Farr Cottage. LT is the one that sent me the staff, well except for Robert who is on staff temporarily while you and Alfred are visiting. Mother and I had a girl that came in to clean once or twice a week, but the house does need work and people to care for it."

Arthur began to speak but Alfred returned. "Were you going to give us the tour? I for one am looking forward to seeing the rest of the house." Turning to Arthur, "Melody is such a wonderful hostess, don't you think?"

Arthur growled. He knew Alfred was comparing the welcome they had received from Melody to the one he had given her when she had visited Farr Cottage. Arthur was about to retort when Melody asked them both to follow her.

"I would love to show you my house." Motioning to the two men, she said, "Come with me, and we'll start with the library."

Melody enjoyed showing the house to the two men, and for the next few hours they went from room to room. Melody told them various things about the people and items with whom each room was associated. The last room was her father's study. The wood paneling, the massive desk, and comfortable chairs were a good stopping point.

"I have so many wonderful memories of my father in this room. This was the desk Richard and his partner in the Newhouse & Farr Bank had used when they originally went into the banking business together. It's one of the few large things that made it through the Storm of 1915, which destroyed the original Farr House. This room means so much to me. And, it is the only room that survived of the house Richard had initially built before he married Miss Lucy."

While the three talked, the miniature grandfather's clock on the mantel chimed eleven o'clock. Quietly, the study door opened, and Bellamy rolled a cart into the room with a decanter of sherry and a cherry cake made especially by Mrs. Bellamy for the visitors. A plate with cake and a small glass of sherry was placed within reach of each person, and Bellamy left as quietly as he had arrived.

Arthur and Alfred looked at each other and nodded. Even though the conversation had continued while Bellamy was in the room, they both noticed the efficiency of the butler. "Melody, you are very fortunate to have such well-trained staff. They are tough to find and in some cases, even more difficult to keep," Arthur said. "I think Alfred would agree."

Alfred laughed. "You've seen my place in London. I have a retired butler who works the few times I need him, but really, no one wants to go into service any longer, at almost any price. It's just too hard to get people anymore who really know what they're doing."

Melody sipped her sherry and took a bite of the cake. It was, at least to Melody's palate, better than any she had had in England. As she looked at her guests, she noticed they were also enjoying the snack.

"Oh, I did want to tell you, LT has invited us all to dinner tonight at his club. LT, my father, and some other men started it years ago to give them a place to have dinner, entertain business people, or take their wives out for a five-star meal. During the week, a business suit is normal, but on Saturday nights it's evening wear." Melody paused. "It is a male-members only club."

Alfred was surprised, "I didn't think there were any "men only" clubs left. I know in Britain it's hard to keep them without the women demanding to be let in. How did this one stay so private?"

Melody laughed, "I think it's probably because of the wives. The men get to have their private club, but the girls get a place where the men have to dress up, the food and service are superb, and the women get to wear their expensive clothes and jewelry. What's not to like? So the men have a private club, the women usually pay the monthly bill and know exactly who he takes there and when. It's a win-win."

Arthur countered, "So you can't take us, only LT or another member?"

"That's right. However, Father was a founding member, and when he died, the membership voted to keep his membership open in case my mother was to re-marry or when I marry." Melody quickly added, "That is, of course, if the man is acceptable to the members."

Arthur and Alfred looked at each other. Of course they would be considered acceptable!

Dinner at the St. Charles was, as usual, a favorite of Melody's. The food and service were excellent and Arthur and Alfred enjoyed it. LT had brought Jeremy, and the three "eligible" gentlemen were beginning to realize they were each up against the other for Melody's attention.

LT's driver brought them all to his apartment at the Chadwick Building after dinner for coffee and brandy. It was the first time Melody had been in the penthouse of the building.

Melody was surprised when she went inside. The house LT's last wife, Sylvia, had helped design had been a mishmash of styles, and the reclaimed barn-wood used on the exterior was carried over, in some instances, into the interior. This apartment, however, had none of that design schizophrenia; it was white, chrome, and glass.

The white leather sofas were comfy, the leather was soft, and the decor radiated LT's personality. A few quite expensive paintings hung on the wall and were the only splashes of color in the main salon. Even the baby grand piano in the corner was white.

Jeremy went to his room to take a call from a Harris cousin, and the other men sat with Melody. When Jeremy returned, he announced he would be joining a group of his cousins for a Friday night poker game the next evening.

LT was quick to jump into the void. "Excellent! I just hope the play doesn't get too rough. I know the group of guys you're playing with. They at least don't play for hotels, hospitals, or apartment blocks." It was then that LT noticed the shocked expressions on everyone's faces. "Relax, the guys who used to do that are my age, and they quit playing poker together back in the 1980s."

"Now," LT continued, "since you are not going to be with us tomorrow night," he motioned to Jeremy then turned to Melody, "what about a barbecue? The weather is supposed to be excellent, and it will be a bit more casual. We have the big charity ball on Saturday, so it might make a nice change."

Melody set her coffee cup on the table. "It sounds good to me." Turning to their lordships, "LT is a grill-master and does wonderful things with meat on the barbecue. If my experience is anything to go by, your jet lag will hit you the hardest tomorrow afternoon, and staying in for a casual dinner might be just the thing."

Both men nodded. Arthur took the initiative. "I agree, but I also think it is time for us to be getting to bed." Turning to Alfred, "I don't know about you, but I'm still running on GMT and could sleep right now. Time to say thank you and goodnight." Alfred nodded his assent.

LT made a call to the garage to have the limo ready. "Then let me walk you all down."

Alfred wasn't up as early as the day before. Arthur and Melody had a chance to eat breakfast alone and went to the library when the meal was finished.

Running her fingers along the edge of her father's old desk, Melody explained to Arthur where the piece had come from. "This was the desk Father used at the bank. He moved it in here when he sold the Farr Bank to the bigger one during the mergers of the 1980s. Great-great-grandfather Ricard Farr had it in his office at the bank after he built the new high rise before the turn of the last century."

"The books," Melody waved her hand to encompass the room, "well, at least the ones they had in the library at the time, had been boxed and put in the round barn to keep them safe during the storm. There have been many additions since then. All in the family were avid readers, but as you can see, this library is not nearly as big as yours at Farr Cottage."

Arthur reached out and took Melody's hand. "My library has been very empty since you left. I can't get any work done. The clock on the mantel ticks too loudly, and Nedda gets on my nerves. Without you, the room, the house, my life is empty. Come back." Arthur looked at the room they were in. "I can see what you have here in this house and the grounds, but you're a Farr and you belong in Farr Cottage with me."

Melody retrieved her hand and lowered her head. "I just don't know. I need time, time to figure out what is best for me and for the future. Believe me when I tell you I have missed you too, but is that enough to make a lasting relationship? As I said, I just don't know. Can …" before Melody could finish what she had started to say, the door to the library opened, and Alfred entered.

Acting as if he had not interrupted anything more than a discussion about books, Alfred wished Arthur and Melody a good morning. "Melody, your cook is fantastic! Her omelets are as light as air and very tasty. Sorry, I missed you both at breakfast, but that last brandy at LT's just put me out. However, I slept well and am ready for the day." Alfred did notice the pained expression on Arthur's face and was sure he was making the older man's life a bit more difficult.

"I don't know about you, Arthur, but this doesn't seem like the big city to me. The quiet of the country is what I feel here in

Melody's home." Turning to Melody, "Do you have horses in the stable? I know I'd be up for a ride on such a beautiful day."

Melody shook her head, "No, we haven't had horses since I went to university. Mother never rode that much, and since I wasn't here, there was no point. By the time I finished graduate school, Mother needed all of my time for her care. I suppose I could ask around and find someplace for us to ride, but it would have to be next week."

"No problem. I'm sure we'll have plenty to do before we return to England. So, what's on for today?" Directing his comment to Arthur, Alfred said, "I'm sure you want to get some rest this afternoon, you know, jet lag and all that."

Arthur was quick to reply, "No, no, I'm fine. I was just looking at Melody's library. I think that, for the age of it, the number of years, well compared to the centuries represented in the Farr Cottage library, the family here has been collecting books, it is rather nice."

Grabbing Melody's hand, "Wonderful, then you'll want to keep yourself busy while Melody shows me the grounds." Before Arthur had a chance to reply, Alfred led Melody out the door and into the gardens.

Making an exasperated expression, "Whew, I thought I'd never get a minute alone with you! So show me around and we can talk."

Arthur could see the couple walking, hand in hand, toward the stable. He thought about following them, but he also wanted to give them some time to chat. Arthur had the feeling Melody did not want to be pushed, and if Alfred were to do that, well, it might just make his case that much stronger.

The morning room also had a good view of the grounds, and Bellamy watched carefully while Alfred walked with Miss Melody. Part of Bellamy's job was to look after his employer, and if anything were to happen to her, Mr. LT would want answers. The conversation between Lord Arthur and Miss Melody in the library did not escape his attention either. Some might consider what he did as eavesdropping; in his line of work, it was simply called efficiency. He was charged with the safety of Miss Melody, and what he was doing was part of the job.

The long-deserted stables turned out to be not so deserted. A mother cat and a litter of kittens had made a home in a couple of forgotten bales of hay. Melody pulled her cell phone out and made a note to call the animal control people to come and get them. Feral cats were a problem in the city, and leaving them there wasn't being kind to them.

For Alfred, the round barn near the stables was an unusual structure, and Melody took a few minutes to explain its origins, the uses to which it had been put, and the stories of some of the people who had used the building. "It was in Miss Lucy's things that I found the diary Annis had kept. The story of her meeting with Chet was so out of the ordinary. But I think it also explained a lot of what happened to them later."

"After the accident, Joseph Lowell made a point of bringing back the dowry Richard had given Annis on her wedding. It contained all of her personal items, like clothing and such, but also her letters, papers, journals, and diaries, and in addition, the cash settlement he had given her on her wedding day. From everything I've read about the family, that was the last contact the Lowell and Farr families ever had. A couple of times Richard, Miss Lucy, Avery, and Constance had gone to take flowers on Annis's birthday, you know, to put on her grave, but none of the Lowells were ever there. Until the Lowell Air Park was sold to a developer in the 1980s, the graves of the Lowell family were on the original Lowell farmland. They were moved to a church the family attended, a Methodist Church, before the golf course was built."

"On Sunday, after church, I'll show you the Farr family plot in the graveyard of the church. They left a place open for Annis and her husband, but the Lowells wanted them buried on their land. Perhaps that was the disagreement that kept the families apart." Melody sighed. She was sure, from the things she had read about the marriage and the interaction of the two families, the fight to have Annis with her family must have been hard fought, but now, what did it matter? Eternity was not always what it seemed when talking about burial plots.

"That is all very interesting and you seem to have a very strong connection to your family and your past," Alfred remarked as he looked around. "I felt you also had a strong connection to life in England, especially to Kent, the Cottage, and our little area of the world."

Alfred took Melody's hands in his. "You know by now how much you mean to me. We have spent hours online talking back and forth, and I don't think there is anything you don't know about me or my life." Looking around at the property and up to the house, "We wouldn't always have to live in England, either at Aldwin House or in London. I'm sure there are seasons of the year when the weather here is much better than at home and vice versa. We can live anywhere you want."

"I don't want you for what you have. I want you for you. I love you, want you, and my life would be complete if you were a part of it. Please, tell me you'll pick me."

Melody pulled her hands away. Hearing that last remark made her wince. "Alfred, this is not a competition. I'm not a reality show, and this is not a Bachelor/Bachelorette type of thing. I'll tell you the same thing I said to Arthur this morning, I need time. Marriage is not something I can take lightly, and it's not just about me. There is a lot to consider, both for now and into the future."

Alfred backed up a step. "I know Arthur wants to marry you, but what about this other fellow, Jeremy. I suppose he is also interested? You say this is not a competition, but for us it is. Only one or none of us will win your hand. I just wanted to let you know my position."

"That's fair enough. As for Jeremy, well, I've only just met him since I came back from England. While I am sure LT has vetted him thoroughly, I don't know that much about him and have spent very little time with him. So, as I said, this is not a competition, I'm not the 'grand-prize,'" and looking at her watch, "now it's time to go back to the house."

"I won't stop pressing my case. You may not see this as a competition, but for me, it is my future and the future of my family. I may not be a viscount, but my family is just as old as the Farr family, and it can't end with me." Alfred took Melody's hand as they walked back toward the house.

Melody turned to him, "What about your circle of friends in England? I'm sure there is one or two of the girls in that group who would like to marry you."

Alfred stopped and looked at the girl by his side. "I have known that bunch all my life or, well, most of it. And yes, any one of them would make me a 'suitable' wife, but if I had wanted one of them, don't you think I would already be married? A group of friends like that usually just, well, eventually, the families start pushing hard enough for us to make whatever matches we can, and we settle for one or another. It's not a love thing but more of a 'who doesn't irritate us more than another'. I don't want that, and I don't think you do either. I want to look forward to being with someone, not just be a wife who is less of a bore than another would be. I want you and I would like you to know that."

A noise drew their attention to the lanai area. Jose` and a man Melody was unfamiliar with were talking loudly about something to do with the pool. Melody apologized to Alfred and told him she would meet him in the library in a few minutes. "I'll think about everything you've just said, I promise. Right now, I want to see what is going on with LT's contractor and the other fellow." Before she dropped Alfred's hand, however, she squeezed it, and gave him a peck on the cheek.

The two men watching from different windows in the house, Bellamy and Lord Arthur, were not happy to see the display of affection between the two. They were, however, happy to see Melody send Lord Alfred back to the house while Melody went to deal with something near the lanai.

Jose` was not happy. While English is a wonderful language for communicating and Jose` and his family had been in the United States from before Texas was a part of America, his family were Texicans and proud of their heritage. The descendants of the original members of his family were all bi-lingual and used Spanish and the expressive words in some very personal situations. Telling a girl you loved her in Spanish was more sensitive than any words of love in English. In the same vein, having an argument in Spanish offered better words and phrases of disdain than the same words in English.

Jose` and the man were having a full-blown row in Spanish when Melody approached them. Jose` put his hands up and motioned to the man he was arguing with that it was time to suspend their disagreement while Melody was in ear-shot. Both men greeted her with a smile.

Although Melody knew quite a bit of Spanish, the fact the argument was in a language other than English showed the men expected the verbal altercation to be between them, and it wasn't her place to hamper their exchange. It was OK for her to ask what was wrong, and if it needed fixing.

"So, Jose`, how is the family?" Without giving him a chance to answer, Melody went on, "I've wanted to tell you how much I appreciate all of the really fine work you and your men have done on the house." Looking around, Melody motioned toward the lanai, "Is there a problem with the outdoor area?"

Before Jose` could speak, the man jumped in, "I'm Mitch from The Backyard Spa. We're the ones who have been asked to redo the pool. I brought a design in and my good friend Jose` here," pointing to man he'd just been in an argument with, "doesn't like the solution I have to your pool refurbishment. Since it's going to be your pool, perhaps you can give your input."

LT had sent Jose` to oversee the work, and Melody didn't want to get in the middle of anything. But she would like to have some say in what was done to her house. Sensing the best thing would be for Jose` to offer her a chance to give her advice, she turned to him. He knew when it was time to bring her into the discussion.

"Miss Melody," Jose` began, "please, you take a look at this design and tell us what you want."

The three went back into the lanai to look at the plans. Mitch had the designs and renderings all laid out on the granite topped bar. "I have two options here. The first one is a quick fix that has a pool reline, updated equipment for controlling the water in the pool, and a redo of the deck around the pool." He pulled a colored rendering out and some other colored photos of tiles and color schemes. "This is what it would look like. Going with the style of the house, Italian or Mediterranean, this tile and color scheme would look the best in my opinion."

Pulling some other drawings out, Mitch went on with his presentation. "The quick fix could be done in a couple of days. The pool liner is top quality and is mold, mildew, and fungus resistant. The color will also not fade for the length of the guarantee."

Mitch pointed to the next group of plans. "This is a mid-term fix and will take longer to do, but it might interest you. We do everything that was done in this group of plans," he patted the pile of papers Melody and Jose` had just been shown, "but it includes the items in this plan. We have designed a new lighting system, some jet sprays, and a rock feature on the other end of the pool away from the bar."

A third set of plans was still in Mitch's portfolio case and he drew them out to show Melody and Jose`. He laid out the plans with a theatrical flair. "This is a total redo of everything, an expansion of the lanai area, and a couple of features with the pool I think you might like. Now, it would take us longer to do, but it will be ready by the time you'll want to use it."

Pointing to the blueprints and renderings, Mitch continued his presentation. "I've looked at the lanai itself, and the screening is in need of replacement anyway so why not take the opportunity to expand and have what you want? Now, anything on this can be done to your liking, but it gives your outside area just about anything you might like. And if you don't see it here, we can put it in."

For the next several minutes the vision of a totally redesigned area was laid before them. The pool would be redesigned from a simple rectangle into an L-shaped affair. The bar would be incorporated into the pool with bar stools in one end of the pool as a "swim-up" feature. The pool itself would have a beautiful array of lights and lighted water jets that would make night swims fun and interesting. The feature that caught Melody's interest the most was the rock grotto in one end of the pool that had a waterfall, which covered the entrance to a private corner with room enough for two people to sit in privacy.

Melody looked at Jose`. "I don't know about you, but this last set of plans, except for the swim-up bar feature, is what I would like to go with. I know it will take more time and be much more expensive, but it is something I think I would really like. Why don't you and Mitch toss it back and forth, clear it with LT, and go with it. I like the darker 'French-blue' for the pool bottom and sides.

This," Melody pointed to a tile and color-scheme palate "would complement the blue and is the one I'd like the most."

Jose` nodded. He would, as always, get the OK from LT before he did anything to Melody's house, but he could see she liked the upgrades. "This is fine with me. It does look like it will make for a very interesting outdoor area. I can't wait to see it done. How long will it all take?"

Mitch checked his notes, "I don't see why it can't be done before Easter, which is late this year and would put it near the end of April. You get your stuff done on the cabana, bar, and outdoor kitchen, and we'll have the pool area done by the time you want to expand and put up the new screening material on the whole thing."

Melody looked at her watch. It was well past eleven, and she had to get to the library for the sherry and cake. "I've got to go. You two do what you do." With that, Melody left to attend to her guests.

Melody had been brought up to believe appointments were given for specific times for a reason. Being late for one was disrespectful, and while there were some people who still believed that being "fashionably late" was acceptable, Melody was never allowed to fall into that practice. With profuse apologies for her tardiness, Melody found her guests in the library waiting for the morning ritual of sherry and cherry cake at eleven.

Bellamy, having watched Melody from one of the windows, timed the arrival of the cart with the cake and sherry perfectly. Both Arthur and Alfred reassured Melody that they understood the reason she was late, and the matter was quickly forgotten. One upside to the entire incident was the sherry. The small amount was just enough to relax both gentlemen, and the jetlag Melody had been expecting would overtake them at any time finally appeared. Less than a half hour after eating the cake and drinking the sherry, Alfred and Arthur excused themselves and went to their respective rooms to take a nap.

Louisa arrived at four to do the final fitting of the ball gown. The dress was still hidden in the long silk bag that had covered it when the consultant first brought it from the vault in the store in New York. Melody had not been using the men's dressing room in her suite up until now, and since it was empty of furniture, it made the perfect place to try on the gown so Louisa could check the waist and length.

Melody stood on a small stool she'd brought into the dressing room from her closet. The height was just enough so Louisa did not have to crawl around on the floor to get to the hem and check the underskirts. The dress was a ball gown in every sense of the meaning, and the two women discussed if it was just a little too ball-gown-ish. The skirt did poof out quite a bit but then perhaps that was better than not enough so they checked. A couple layers of the underskirts were removed to see what it would look like, but both decided the full effect of the gown was better left as the designer had intended.

Before Louisa left, Melody took out the necklace and earrings LT had brought Melody from the vault at the bank. The gold filigree, diamonds, and sapphires looked like they were made to go with the outfit. After a few moments, she decided the faux-fur she had worn with the red dress would have to do for the ball.

Melody walked Louisa to the door and was in time to greet LT as he arrived to start the grill. Their lordships were still napping, and LT recommended they be left to sleep off the jetlag for as long as possible. Their absence would give him a chance to talk to Melody alone, something which hadn't been possible since Jeremy, and now Arthur and Alfred, always seemed to be in attendance.

The first and most important order of business, however, was the grill, and once it was started, LT could sit with Melody and enjoy an end-of-day whisky at the outdoor bar. Melody laid out the pool drawings and plans for LT to see.

"I like this idea," LT started, "but what if this" pointing to the L-shape "was moved over here." LT looked around for a pencil. "I need a pencil, something to draw with. Bellamy!" he called.

Like any good butler, Bellamy was in earshot of his employer and her guest, and hearing Mr. LT's voice he came to see what service he could provide. "Yes, sir?"

LT told Bellamy what he wanted and within a couple of minutes, a small selection of drawing instruments was at hand. "OK. Now, if this was moved over here, forget the L-shape, make it more of a squat T. Put the waterfall and grotto here, but make the top of the waterfall a diving platform and make the pool deep enough here to dive safely. Hmm, and here, this will give you a lot more room to have sofas, chairs, and tables for … uh … for … oh, what did Sylvia call those things?! Oh, right, "conversation" areas. Yep, I like it! I think it's great, but," an idea seemed to flash into LT's head, "a water slide, what would make this place the best is a water slide."

LT was quickly sketching an oddly shaped object. "See, they will be using faux-rocks here," he pointed to the grotto and water-fall, "they can do the same thing here with the waterslide. This will be one special pool. One of a kind probably. I'll talk to Jose` tomorrow and have him get started right away."

Melody looked at the plans for her pool. The area under the lanai would be double of what it was now. She liked what LT had done, and the water slide was fine. However, it was going to need some plants to soften the hardness of the rocks. Fake or not, they were a little starker than she wanted. "I like it, but it needs some plants and stuff to give it that "oasis" feel. Don't you think?"

LT nodded. "I'll make sure plants are included in the design." Turning from the designs on the bar top, LT motioned Melody inside to the study. "Why don't you and I visit for a bit before your friends get up?"

Melody led the way and sat in her father's chair. Bellamy refilled LT's whiskey and poured a Scotch for his employer. "Shall I have Robert waken their lordships?"

Melody looked at LT. She knew he wanted to talk to her about something and so she shook her head. "No Bellamy. I'd like you to wait another half-hour before you wake them. LT and I have some things to discuss." Quietly, Bellamy left the room.

"So," Melody began, "what did you want to talk about?"

LT sipped at his drink, looked at his watch and set his drink down. "How's the visit, anything new going on?"

Melody chuckled. "Nothing new. Arthur and Alfred are just napping off the jetlag. Robert has sent their evening clothes out to be pressed before tomorrow. And yes, both of them have asked me, well in a roundabout way, asked me to marry them. And before you get all excited, I've told both of them I wanted, needed, time to think about it." Melody sipped her scotch. "Is that what you wanted to know about?"

LT checked his watch again and laughed. "OK, maybe it seems like I'm anxious, but I just want to make sure everything is going along alright. Don't be too hard on me. I've never met these guys before and I don't know what kind of men they are. I expect to give you away when you get married, and I won't give you away to someone I have to worry about."

"OK, fair enough." Melody saw LT check his watch for a third time. "Do you have to be somewhere? You keep looking at your watch like you need to run out of here at any moment."

LT laughed. "No, girl, I'm checking the time for the grill! I have no place to be but here this evening."

Melody called to Bellamy. When the butler entered, "Please light the fire-pit. LT is never going to relax until he is sitting where he can watch the grill."

LT and Melody picked up their drinks, Melody grabbed a jacket, and the two headed out to the grill area. LT immediately started checking the grill and moved some of the coals around with the long tongs.

Bellamy had positioned the portable fire-pit near the grill and placed a couple of extra chairs around it for their lordships when they would join Miss Melody and LT. Before he left the lanai, Bellamy refilled the drinks.

LT sat next to Melody so they could talk. "Is it warm enough for you?" Melody nodded. "Good. One of the things I wanted to tell you was that I found you a car, and it will be here tomorrow, probably in the morning."

Melody gave him a quizzical look. "LT, you already sent that big SUV over a couple of weeks ago. It seems fine to me. What do I need another car for?"

"Now, now, just hear me out. It's used, but only has a little over thirty-five hundred miles on it. It's charcoal-gray, and I think you'll love it. Bellamy can drive you to the charity ball in it tomorrow night."

Melody looked at LT sideways. "OK. It sounds really nice, but you're not telling me something. What's wrong with it? Has it been in a major accident? Or, flooded, oh no," Melody's voice sounded alarmed, "it's from Seattle where they just had those flash floods, right? Please, tell me it hasn't been flooded!"

"Calm down," LT needed to reassure Melody. "There is nothing wrong with it. It's actually from Tulsa. The man that had the car found he didn't like it as much as he thought he would so he put it on the market. It hasn't been in a wreck, flooded, or anything like that. If anything, it has been cared for like a part of the family."

Melody relaxed. LT continued. "I, well, it's a Rolls that is about four years old. The guy who is selling it got it for his mother, and when she passed away, thought he would keep it for himself.

But, he just isn't the Rolls kind of guy. I think you are, and it was such a good deal. Well, I think it will still be in service and taking your grandchildren to their proms or weddings."

A Rolls, hmm, Melody had to think about that one. "I thought when you said you were getting me a car, it would be like Grandmother's. Why not an American-made car like the one she had?"

"Because dear girl, they don't make them anymore. I looked at Lincoln. That's what your gran had, and at Cadillac, both have downsized the luxury cars to the place you have to have them modified in specialty shops to get a true limo. You know, the places where they make those stretch limos that are tricked out with drink bars and stripper-poles."

Melody laughed. "No, I don't want a stretch anything. Of course, the bar does sound nice, but I don't think that's what you're talking about." Sighing in resignation, "Well, if that is what you've gotten me, then I guess it's OK. However, who will take care of it? Doesn't it take a special kind of mechanic to do the work on those things?"

LT laughed. "Yes, and I've talked to Tommy Hernandez about it already. His cousin Frank has a shop near his that does only foreign cars. He is qualified to work on it, or there is the dealership over on Gulf Freeway that can take care of the car. This is, however, not something about which you need to worry. The care of the cars is in Bellamy's very capable hands. He is your driver as well as your butler, so he is the one that will make sure your vehicles are kept at their best."

Melody nodded, much of her day-to-day stuff had been taken over by other people. She no longer had to take her dry-cleaning, pick up mail, pay bills, or do grocery shopping. A couple times, she had stopped at a store to get something only to find it was already in the kitchen or the fridge. Since then, she has just gone with what the staff has so capably done.

"Was the car the only thing? Oh, that and to keep tabs on who was trying to marry me?" Melody had to hide her smile. "There must be more."

LT laughed. "Well, there is, but it's nothing, really. It's just… well … I gave you my staff thinking I wouldn't need anybody full-time in the penthouse. I have a maid who comes and cleans while I'm at the office. I've only seen her once, but she does good work." LT took the last sip of his whiskey. "I eat out way too much, but I guess I could get someone to come in and cook for me. What I really want is someone on a permanent basis. This is why I have asked Bellamy to recommend someone."

As if by magic, Bellamy was at LT's elbow taking his empty glass and replacing it with a full one. Motioning to Melody's butler, "See, this is what I want. I miss it. So, as I said, I've asked Bellamy, and he thinks Robert, your temporary under-butler might do just fine for me."

Melody looked at Bellamy, "Miss Melody, we will only need Robert while their lordships are here, and after that, he might make a good fit in Mr. LT's establishment."

Melody smiled as she addressed Bellamy. "I think that's a great idea. Does he cook? I hope so, or LT is going to find his five-bedroom penthouse has become a very crowded place with maids, butlers, and cooks." Tasting her new drink, "Oh, and I think it's time to get the visitors up for drinks and dinner. Please ask Robert to wake them and tell them it is casual for this evening. Tonight it's drinks on the patio!"

The men must have already been up because they both appeared in less than five minutes. The traditional "drinks before dinner" was timed just about right. LT announced the meat would be ready in a half hour, and Mrs. Bellamy had the other items to go with it prepared to be served when the barbecue was finished.

Bellamy made drinks for everyone, and the two Englishmen, used to bundling up against the chill, were quite happy to be outside in front of the fire-pit. While LT saw to the grill, the conversation swirled around the wonderful naps the two men enjoyed and a declaration by both that their jetlag was in the past.

Alfred was especially talkative, and the before-dinner drinks were accompanied by a funny story he told. Melody watched Arthur while Alfred was talking, and it did appear the two men could be in the same room without the animosity she had seen in England. Arthur's face wasn't quite as sour when Alfred was speaking.

The group ate their dinner in the more informal breakfast room. Instead of being served a filled plate for each course by Bellamy, dishes of vegetables, bread, and condiments were put on the table, and people helped themselves. The two different meats LT had made on the barbecue were tasty without any additional seasonings, and the vegetables Mrs. Bellamy made complemented the food quite well.

LT looked at Lord Arthur and asked about his work. "Melody tells me you are some kind of specialist historian called a "book." Haven't you found yourself being replaced by computers? I know most of the information people want can be found there. How does that affect you?"

Arthur laid his fork down and took a sip of wine. "I understand the confusion some people might have about what it is I actually do. When I was up at Oxford, I found a don who helped me use my photographic memory. It was somewhat strange for me. I had grown up with a keen memory, but I thought everyone was that way. I didn't think I was special, but this man not only informed me of how wrong that idea was but showed me how to use what I did have in a most advantageous way."

LT wanted to know more. "OK, what is a "don" and what did he show you about using your memory?"

Arthur smiled. "Sorry, I suppose here you would call a don a university fellow or tutor. Anyway, it is all about sorting what I do know. Every time I read a journal article, book, monograph, or other kind of writing, I sort it into various places in my mind by making connections to other things I already knew. The reason I can do something most computers can't is this connection function. It's like pulling a thread and finding what is attached to it."

LT nodded. "That I understand, but Melody said you did this for several of your government's ministries. Sounds like steady work."

Arthur and Alfred both laughed, but Arthur continued. "I get enough to keep me busy, but nothing having to do with government work in my country pays well. My family has an extremely long tradition of serving our king, well in this case queen, but I think you get my meaning. I don't do it for the money. I do it because that is what the people of my family do."

LT chuckled. "Fair enough. There have been times when I have been asked to sit on boards or commissions for the public good and was never paid for the "privilege"."

Melody wanted to get away from the subject of people's work. She had a feeling LT was fishing for information she figured he already had documented. Melody was sure LT had ordered complete background checks on both of her guests, and the information gathered would have included financial statements. LT probably knew to the penny what each man was worth, what had been passed to them from their family's estates/titles, and how they earned their money.

What Melody had not foreseen was the fact that Arthur wanted to talk about his situation, possibly because he wanted to let LT know he was more than able to take care of Melody if she agreed to marry him. He also wanted LT and Alfred to know he wasn't after her for her inheritance.

"LT," Arthur started, "my family goes back to before the Norman invasion and the subjugation of my Anglo-Saxon family by William, the bastard duke of Normandy. We have always served our kings as knights, and later, after the Restoration of Charles II, as the Viscount of Gibbons. The family has been fortunate not to have had the hard luck of suffering from spendthrifts, drunkards, nor gamblers in our lineage. None of the family has spent money on loose women or other distractions as other of the old families in my country have. I must also say the same is true of the Oswin family, but then I'm sure Alfred will speak for himself on this subject."

Arthur waved his hand around the room for effect. "What Melody's family has built here is a testament to the stability of our line. Even though her great-great-grandfather could not inherit under the laws of succession, he came to a new world and built a new life. It really is quite impressive what he accomplished. In many families, non-inheriting sons simply wasted what little they had or, even worse, became a burden on the part of the family that did inherit. Richard was exceptional."

Continuing in a more sarcastic vein, Arthur said, "Some of our *wonderful* Labour governments have tried to end what Alfred and I are and represent. Death and inheritance taxes are being used to destroy the great estates and diminish the influence of the titled class. Part of that is how titles are passed down in families. I am the last of the direct male line of Farrs, but Melody here," motioning to his ward, "is my closest relative. If I were to die without issue, she would have not just her estate to deal with but mine as well. She would, well, if she were in England, inherit the title with it."

The people at the table grew silent. Alfred entered the conversation and added his points. "Yes, since the new generation in the royal family has started having little princes and princesses, the old queen decided to change the laws to let a female of the line inherit the throne. When Kate was first preggers, the gossip pages were full of the "well, what if it's a girl?" chatter. Buckingham Palace, always aware they needed to stay relevant to modern British life, put it out that whatever the sex of the first-born child, they would be next in line to the throne. Parliament passed the *succession* bill, and although the first was a boy and there was no need for the bill, it did take the "only boys can inherit" restriction off of titles as well."

"I'm also the last of my line, well, supposedly," Alfred looked at Arthur, "it might not be the case if certain people would admit to certain possibilities." Arthur squirmed. "But for right now, I'm in the same place as Arthur, all alone with no one to take over the estate and title."

Bellamy came into the room and silently started taking the empty plates away. Melody needed to break the mood. Directing her comments to her butler, "We'll have coffee and brandy in the study." Then, looking at the men at the table, "Shall we leave and let the staff clean up?"

Saturday morning finally arrived. It was a beautiful day for early December, and the temperatures were mild. Melody had everything ready for the big charity ball, and whatever the other attendees were doing, it didn't affect her.

Gina came for a visit late in the morning and joined Melody and her guests for the traditional sherry and cake. One late arrival, LT, urged everyone to follow him to the front portico.

There, stately and classically lined, was Melody's car. The Rolls was everything LT had described to her. Bellamy came and sat in the front seat and checked the instrument panel, adjusted the mirrors, and opened the glove box to examine the papers. He would be the driver, and it was up to him to learn all he could about the new addition to the garage.

LT opened the door for Melody and Gina to sit in the back seat. The men stood around and admired the fine workmanship that was a hallmark of Rolls Royce. Arthur was the first to speak. "A well-cared for Rolls will last someone a lifetime. This looks like a keeper. And," directing his comment to Melody with an impish grin, "it looks good on you."

Melody still wasn't too sure about going into this much luxury for a car. Gina kidded her, "Hey, if you don't want it…" The girls laughed about it.

"OK, I guess since it's already been paid for it can stay. My garage has been rather empty since first Grandmother's, then Mother's and my cars were taken out. It left only Father's college car and the new SUV. I feel like we've just adopted a pet or something." Melody smiled as she caressed the fine leather. "The seats are so comfortable, they make you feel "wanted"."

By the time the driver from the dealership who had brought the car was picked up, Gina felt it was time for her to go home and start getting ready for the big party. LT left to get something Jeremy had asked for at the shoe store, and their lordships retired to their respective rooms. LT was picking them up on his way back to his penthouse, and they would leave for the ball from there.

It left Melody to come alone in her new car driven by Bellamy. Melody thanked LT. He knew she wanted to keep her dress a secret until she arrived at the event, and by taking her guests with him, it was making her "reveal" easier to arrange. She just had to be at the ball on time but get there after the men from her table had arrived.

Rodney, the director of Mr. LT's security office at Chadwick Holdings, arrived at Melody's home just before Bellamy was to bring the car from the garage. Rodney handed Bellamy a brown envelope with the logo of a medical lab printed on the front.

Bellamy turned it over and saw the stamp on the flap showing the seal was still intact.

"Is this what I think it is?" Bellamy asked as he put the envelope into his suit coat pocket.

Rodney nodded. "Yep, LT wanted it ASAP, and it was couriered over just now. Since you are seeing him in a few minutes, I figured you could slip it to him without anyone being the wiser. Oh, and enjoy the party!" The men shook hands and Rodney left.

Robert had accompanied their lordships to LT's penthouse to assist them in preparing for the ball. It also gave LT a chance to sit and talk to the young under-butler and ask Robert if he would like to come to work at LT's apartment. Robert eagerly agreed.

LT, the two English visitors, and Jeremy left for the party. Robert rode in the front seat and would park Melody's car when she arrived with Bellamy. Robert and Bellamy would take the car home again and wait for the call to return and get Miss Melody and their lordships from the charity ball.

LT led his guests into the party. The charity was for the hospital that the Harris side of the family had started under Dr. John Harris back in the late 1800s. From a small clinic, it had grown into an institution that was an integral part of the Houston Medical Center. It stood proud among such world-renowned names as M. D. Anderson, Baylor, UTMB, and Memorial/Hermann. The hospital's work on diabetes, gangrene, and kidney problems associated with diabetes put it at the forefront on medical research into the problems caused by diabetes.

Each year, the George R. Brown Convention Center was decorated with bunting, flowers, and ice sculptures for the big event. Tables were sold for several thousands of dollars, all for the charity. A silent auction also brought in funds, and a "first dance" auction was held to liven up the evening. Besides the extensive network of Harris, Chadwick, Higgins, and Lopez cousins, the business and society leaders of Houston were in attendance to mark the final ball of the charity season.

LT had a table for twelve. Marsha, LT's secretary, had sent the instructions on the location of the place cards, but they had to be repositioned to his liking. Gina and her escort were seated near Melody who would sit at the right-hand of LT. Next to her, he put Lord Arthur, then Lord Alfred, and at his own left-hand, LT put Jeremy. May Harris-Chadwick, the widow of Michael Chadwick an aged aunt of LT, was seated next to Jeremy. George Chadwick, brother to LT, and his wife were seated next to Lord Alfred, and the last couple, Judy and Louise Chadwick, older sisters of LT, rounded out the table.

Bellamy pulled the car under the portico of the venue for the ball. A carpet led from the curb to the entrance and a "red-carpet" atmosphere permeated the crowd gathered to watch the people as they went inside. A couple of photographers were there, freelancers who would sell their pictures to the local paper or one of the television stations.

The crowd saw the beautiful elegance of the Rolls and understood it might be holding someone of great importance. The car wasn't flashy enough for a rock-star or sports figure, but who could it be? Robert walked up to the car and opened the door for Melody to emerge. Jeremy, in his full Evening-Dress "A" Marine uniform, stepped forward to hand Melody from the car.

The faux-fur jacket hid the top of the dress; but the full ball skirt, dainty satin pumps, and the jewels she wore around her neck and hanging from her ears made an instant impression. Before having their photos taken by the waiting photographers, Melody took off the jacket and handed it to Jeremy to hold. He stepped back to get the full effect of this radiant girl.

Like the two men waiting inside, Melody's beauty hit Jeremy in an instant. Her height absolutely made the dress. If she had been any shorter, the gown would have overwhelmed her. Her stature and also her curves, which filled it out in all the right places, and the confidence she exuded were all in evidence. The color, a deep, dark, pure blue, was shot through with iridescent threads that made the material flow with every move Melody made. Light bulbs flashed several times before Jeremy claimed her and led her into the ballroom.

LT watched as the young couple stood on the red carpet. For Melody to have found that dress, the trip to New York was worth every penny and every minute. He had seen the bill come through on her account, and as far as he was concerned, she had made a bargain.

When Bellamy had pulled the car up to let Miss Melody get out, Robert was there to open the door and then take the car to park it temporarily. Bellamy moved to the side of the carpet and caught LT's eye as LT stood admiring Melody's arrival. A barely perceptible nod on Bellamy's part let LT know he needed a word with him.

Without saying anything, Bellamy pulled the envelope from his inside coat pocket and handed it to LT who smiled and nodded a "thank you" to Bellamy. LT had been waiting for this but didn't want to open it in public. As soon as he could excuse himself, he would read the contents in the men's room.

Jeremy handed Melody's jacket to a coat-check girl. Taking her arm, he took her to where LT was standing. Before he got to the older man, however, the two English visitors had also come to see Melody. LT beamed at his goddaughter, and the other men simply stood, awestruck.

At the dinner party hosted by Lord Alfred in London, Melody had been a stunner in a dove-gray charmeuse silk dress that fit her like a second skin. Both Lord Alfred and Lord Arthur had realized their feelings for her that night, but the dress she wore to the charity ball put the gray dress in an "also ran" category.

LT looked around and saw the men at his table were not the only ones admiring Melody. Some of those other men he recognized, but one or two were new to him. He would have to be careful about Melody when it came to the auction for the first dance. Before the festivities could begin, however, he slipped away to the men's lounge to examine the contents of the report Bellamy had slipped to him earlier.

It wasn't a lengthy paper. The results of the DNA tests were given with a probability of 99.9 percent accuracy. LT smiled and wondered what the other fraction of a percent was and realized it was the lab's way of covering its ass in the event the report had, in any way, been faulty. At 100 percent the people doing the work could be sued if it was found to be wrong. However, for LT, it was the answer he wanted to have, and finally, the argument of a familial relationship between the House of Farr and the House of Oswin could be settled.

Back in the ballroom, LT's table was a center of motion. Several people were coming to find out who the girl was, introduce themselves, and for some of the young men, try to strike up a conversation. The orchestra was playing an introductory piece that should have been a signal for everyone to find their seats, quiet down, and let the first speaker introduce the evening.

LT made sure everyone was seated in the right place at his table, and then he too sat down next to Melody. He leaned over and told her how good she looked and said, "I know your mom and dad would have been so proud of you. You look fabulous, and those jewels are perfect for that dress and for you."

Melody whispered back, "Oh, Pinky, thank you for setting this up. It looks like it will be a fairy-tale night!"

The room finally fell silent, and one of LT's older cousins, Dr. Bartholomew J. Harris, head of Medical Research at St. Luke's Anglican Hospital, welcomed the guests. Silently, the waiters and waitresses were moving around the room, putting the dinner plates, salads, and drinks on the tables so the dinner could begin. Another cousin of LT's, the socialite wife of one of the doctors at the hospital who had arranged the charity ball, was introduced. She explained to everyone the silent auction, the "first dance" auction, and quipped, "We hope you all have brought your checkbooks because we will be collecting donations later on. Remember, we're not going to let you go home until we meet our goal!" It was a sentiment the room laughed at but understood was not completely a joke.

Conversation flowed around the table, and LT watched as Melody, Jeremy, and their lordships interacted. There were times when he wished the girl didn't have as many choices or that having more than one husband was not a possibility. Lord Arthur had the name, Jeremy would protect the girl, and Alfred seemed to be a good choice also. Knowing what he now knew, well, it was going to make the way he leaned a little iffy. If the science was right, then there was…

Melody nudged LT's arm, leaned close, and whispered apprehensively, "Pinky, pay attention, they've started the "first dance" auction. Somebody I don't know is bidding to dance the first dance with me. Who is he?"

LT put his thoughts in the back of his mind. He would think about that later. Coming back to full attention, he looked where Melody indicated. Their lordships and Jeremy were looking upset. Apparently, someone was bidding a hefty sum to claim a first dance with Melody. None of the men at the table had come prepared for such a situation, and they were all looking to LT for some guidance.

LT raised his hand and outbid the stranger. "Now, Mike, you wouldn't begrudge me the chance to have the first dance with my goddaughter would you? I promise, if she is so inclined and you can get a slot in her dance card, well, you can have a turn around the floor with her." The room chuckled.

Mike Lowell, a distant cousin of Chet and Hal Lowell, blushed slightly and grinned. "Aw LT, I guess that's OK, but I do hope Miss Farr will give me a dance before the night is over."

LT was happy to have that problem avoided. Before he could go back to his musings, the music began, and the ladies and their partners who had won their first dances took to the floor.

The first dance was traditionally a waltz, and LT twirled Melody around the floor. They had barely made one circuit of the ballroom when Jeremy stepped up and took her from her godfather. Not to be out done, Alfred and Arthur jostled for their turn.

While Melody was on the dance floor, LT stood at the bar getting a refill on his drink. People came and went, and some asked him about the young lady. Melody hadn't been out in public very much before this and mostly only as part of charity work for the church. More than one inquired about her marital status for either themselves or a male relative.

Looking around the room at the interest in his goddaughter, LT was convinced if Melody stayed in Houston too much longer, the marriage market for her would begin to heat up a bit more than he had wanted. Perhaps it was better for her to go back to England sooner than he had planned. The English guys were leaving after New Year, but he needed her to stay until at least the middle of January.

Hmm, and what about Lord Arthur? Since he is now interested in her, is he still the best guardian for her? And, well yes, "and," what about the DNA results? No, he needed some time to work through this, and now was not the best time.

LT walked to his table, set down the partially finished drink, and asked Honey Lee Parker for a dance. The bleached-blond divorcee of former Astros outfielder Chip Parker was totally uncomplicated and a good dancer. He might even ask her back to the penthouse for a drink but then remembered Jeremy was staying with him. As he moved Honey Lee around the floor in a *Texas-two-step*, he smiled at the luck of having Jeremy as a check on his iffier evening's plans. Getting too close to anyone right now might not be the best thing for him.

Near the end of the evening, when the orchestra was on its last break before playing the final few dances, LT had a chance to talk to Melody. He could tell by the glow in her face she was having a wonderful time.

"Well, girl," LT started, "have you enjoyed yourself?"

"Oh, Pinky, you know I have. The only time I've had a chance to sit down since the dancing started was during the breaks for the silent auction, the orchestra's intermissions, and one time when I slipped away to the ladies' lounge. It's a good thing these shoes are comfortable!"

"It looks like you've had a dance with every person in the place. Maybe you'll save the last dance for me," LT said with a big grin but then turned serious. "I, uh, I've been thinking. Maybe it would be better if you went back to England as you had first planned. Jose` has the work at the house well in hand. You've chosen the designs for the pool and gardens, so I just can't think what more you could get done here. What do you say?"

Melody was puzzled. "What, can't wait to get rid of me? Hmm, I didn't think you'd get tired of having me around so soon."

LT vigorously shook his head. "No, no, it's nothing like that. I love having you here, however, these next few months I've got some very important work to do in the Far East, and I won't be here. I think it would be good if you would at least be with your guardian if you can't be with me, the trustee. We don't want to break the letter or the spirit of your dad's will. No, I think it would be best if you were in England."

"There is one thing, though," LT started to speak, but before he could continue, Lord Arthur came to claim a dance with Melody.

Before LT could stop her, Melody told her cousin about the change of plans. Lord Arthur beamed. "We have missed you, er … well, I've missed you. Having you back home will be just grand. Yes, just grand," He said as he led her onto the dance floor. As they whirled around in a waltz, the iridescent threads in the blue of the dress twinkled like stars in an evening sky. They made a lovely couple, but then that could be said of her and Jeremy or her and Lord Alfred.

LT patted his pocket. Tomorrow, or the next day, he would decide what to do with the results Bellamy had given him. Right now, he looked forward to dancing with his goddaughter. He supposed he would just have to think about the day when he would dance at her wedding and how to see to the extension of the Farr line into the future. It seemed that now, it was up to him.

Farr House

Characters by Location or Time

Home in Houston

Melody Fitzhugh Farr – daughter of the late Charles Andrew Farr and Evangeline Louis Fitzhugh

Gina Russell – Melody's best friend.

LT (Lionel Tyrone) Chadwick (Pinky) – Head of Chadwick Holdings, Melody's late father's best friend, Trustee of the father's estate, which is being held in trust for Melody, and Melody's godfather.

LT's children – Mike who is in a medical residency program and Sally who is becoming a nun.

LT's ex-wives – Celia, Margarete, Linda, and Shirley

Rev. Erick Grey – Anglican priest at St. John's church

Lisa Grey – wife of the Rev. Erick Grey

Jeremy Luke Higgins – great-great-grandson of George Adam Higgins, brother of the original Jeremy Higgins, best friend and mentor of Richard Farr. Currently he is serving as a captain in the U. S. Marine Corps.

Lord Arthur Roland Farr – Viscount of Gibbons– cousin and guardian of Melody Fitzhugh Farr lives in Farr Cottage, the family's ancestral home in Kent, England

Lord Alfred Oswin – lives at Aldwin House near Farr Cottage – Father Sir Alden Alfred Oswin – Mother Lady Mayda Elizabeth Fitzwilliam

Staff in Farr Cottage

Nedda – the housekeeper

John – husband of Nedda and serves as driver, butler, gardener

Lily – day help in Farr Cottage, lives in the village

Staff of Farr House

Tommy Hernandez – man whose family was responsible for caring for the Farr family's cars

Bellamy – former special forces, worked for LT more than ten years

Mrs. Bellamy – wife of Bellamy, cook/chef

Glenda and Pauline – like to be called Glen and Paul, sisters, originally from England, maids

Robert Latrell – hired part-time to care for their lordships during their stay and was later hired full-time to work for LT in his penthouse

Jose` and his brothers – LT's builders

Mitzy Feirst – Interior designer

Louisa – Melody's dressmaker and tailor

Annis's Story

Annis Louis Farr – daughter of Ricard and Lucy Farr, twin sister of Avery

    Chester Lowell – husband of Annis

    Hector Lowell – twin brother of Chester Lowell

    Joseph Lowell – father of the Lowell twins

Avery – Annis's twin brother

Constance Juliet Howard of Richmond, Virginia, wife of Avery and niece of Greg Howard

Doctor John Harris (Doc) – founder of St. Luke's Anglican Hospital

Elbeth Chadwick Harris – wife of Doc Harris and mother of Alice, John Jr., Fred, Lois, Hank, Gillian, Judy, Marsha, Harry, and Tom

Jeremy Higgins – Best friend of Richard Farr, mentor, and husband of the late Abbey Higgins, aunt of Annis and Avery's mother Lucinda (Miss Lucy) Louise Langley Farr. Godfather of Annis and Avery.